CONFESSIONS of a BOOMTOWN MADAM

MARCY WALDENVILLE

Printed in the United States of America
First Printing, 2014

Cover Photos by Shutterstock.
Cover Design by Blue-Eyed Dog Publications.

Dedicated to the Bad Girls with the hearts of gold:

Inara Sara
Kitty Russell
Irma La Douce
Vivian Ward
And Miss Belle Watling
Girls, this one's for you!!!

Acknowledgements

I want to thank the following people:

The Mayhem Sisters, S.K. McClafferty and J.D. Wylde for their encouragement and wisdom.

And Kenny Waldenville, who makes all things possible.

A Message to the Reader

Twenty years ago, my mother found a journal in the attic of her mother's house. Colton Manor, where my mother grew up was to pass to the current Earl of Carrick, more commonly known as boring cousin Arty.

The old book was cracked and dusty and some wretched bug had worked through a portion of it, but it was readable. However, the subject matter had shocked my conservative mother. She had read it cover to cover, however, and put it away, swearing never to open "that repulsive thing" again.

The moment she deemed it unreadable, I became obsessed with it. But it had mysteriously disappeared. It wasn't until my sister and I were cleaning out the attic of our mother's house that I found the journal again. I immediately reverted to a twelve-year-old. I hid it from Claudia and took it home to finally get a look inside.

Inside the cover was a name I had never heard before, Maggie McGregor, and it was dated 1879-1885. My curiosity took over and I began to carefully read the fragile pages and the story came alive for me.

A few days later I talked to my cousin, Michael, about who this mysterious woman was, why her lurid story was in my mother's attic, why it had set her teeth on edge and yet, why she hadn't just thrown the thing out?

Who was this Maggie McGregor?

Michael, the family archivist, was very excited. He reminded me that our twice great grandmother's name was Margaret Grant, the Countess of Carrick. This made me laugh out loud. I doubted this tale was one of a Royal Society heiress.

Michael went on to tell me that Margaret was a buccaneer, an American, who had traveled to London and met our twice great-grandfather, the notorious rogue, Conner Grant, at the height of the season in 1885.

An American? But surely this woman, this Maggie, couldn't be the beloved society matron who had dined with royals, never missed a speech by her husband at parliament, and rigidly adhered to the slightest rule of propriety or decorum?

Michael said that there had been talk, whispers that she was a woman with a past. She had been some sort of railway heiress and her money, along with her husband's solid reputation had stopped the tongues from wagging until she had established herself in society.

Well, the pieces came together. A long held family secret had landed in my lap. I began to tell Michael about the journal. I explained to him, my studious, bookworm of a cousin that the roots of our, oh-so-proper British family, ran right through a western American saloon madam. I could actually hear him fretting through the phone.

He wanted to know what I was going to do next. I thought about it for a long time and then turned it over to a friend of mine, trusting her to tell the story in a way that was honest, straightforward and as to the point as possible.

This is Maggie's story.

Thank you,

Colleen Armstrong

Part One

The Beginning

May 22, 1879

I'm not sure when I lost my innocence. Most people would have said the day Deacon Harris bent me over his desk, lifted my skirts and took my virginity. But I think it was years earlier; when my father died, leaving my mother, my sister and I with little or no hope for a happy future....

Maggie sat behind the desk staring past John's head at the horses frolicking in the field. Oh, how she envied them their freedom. She had no such thing, had not had it in a very long time. She had work and other people's children but not freedom, not a life of her own. Still her mother sent her letters reminding her to be grateful. That was the most bitter pill of all.

What did she have to be grateful for? She was soon out of a job for the summer and there was no money left for her to live off of, which reminded her how hungry she was. Her stomach growled and John's head came up. His dark greasy hair fell over his beady eyes and he gave her a toothy grin.

"Have you finished the assignment?" she asked curtly. He was supposed to be writing "I will not spit on the floor" fifty times.

"Yea," the boy said.

"Yes, Ma'am." Maggie reminded him, only for the fourteenth time that day.

"Yes, ma'am," he repeated, more mockingly than necessary. "Can I go home? My mom got a roasted chicken and sweet potatoes, fresh bread and strawberry preserves waiting for me."

Maggie's stomach growled again, and the little bastard grinned. He was the sort of kid she would catch pulling the wings off of flies and hitting the smaller children with a stick. She hated him.

"Go."

He scrambled out of the chair and ran. Maggie was still thinking about the roast chicken as she gathered her things and locked the door to the small school house outside Willet, Ohio.

She was staying with the Carter Family this week. It was common practice for small towns to share the care and feeding of a teacher to keep from having to provide a house or an income above five dollars a month. No one wanted to have to pay more, so she was passed around like a poor relation.

And she was supposed to be grateful for that?

The worst part was that most women thought you were there to lighting their chore load, as though pounding something into their little brats' heads wasn't enough. And some of the men thought you were there to slake their lust. As if she would willingly give herself to some ignorant hayseed.

She wasn't grateful for that either. So she stayed to herself as much as possible this last week of school and spent some of her hard-earned pennies on a coach ride back to New Philadelphia.

Her mother reminded her constantly that she was still young and pretty enough to find a man to marry. But she hated the thought of explaining her lack of virginity to any man. The sort of man she might want to marry was the sort to hold her past against her. And the sort of man that didn't care was not the sort she wanted.

She was stuck, unless she found a way to make her own money. She was sick of being hungry and having her plain dresses hang on her skinny frame.

Home was not as much of a blessing as it had been when Maggie was a child. After her father had died, the farm and stock he had worked so hard to build were sold off. Most of the money had gone to pay his debts, the rest to buy a small but respectable house in town, and a meager yearly stipend for her mother to live on. Alma McGregor had been the daughter of a banker and had married a gentleman farmer and horse breeder. She was ill-equipped for work and had made a fuss over having to take care of her small house and children, let alone bend her back to any incoming earning work.

It had fallen on sixteen-year-old Maggie to figure out how to make the money stretch. When Laird Harris, Deacon of the First Baptist Church suggested to her mother that he, as headmaster of a local teaching academy, might be able to get Maggie and her younger sister, Grace, teaching positions, he had not mentioned the cost until Maggie had agreed to meet him in his office. He had locked the door, given Maggie a speech about the temptations of a woman's flesh, then grabbed her, bend her forward over his desk, torn her bloomers and shoved his hard dick into her.

Maggie had been too shocked and terrified to even call out in pain. When he was done, he forced her to her knees to pray with him and then threatened her that if she opened her mouth he would do the same to her fourteen-year-old sister. Maggie had stumbled to her feet, clutching the desk in horror when he smiled and told her he expected her to come to his office once a week, or she and her sister would be out on the street.

She had tried to tell her mother what had happened, but the right words had never come. And any time she mentioned Deacon Harris, her mother rattled off the long list of reasons why they were all so indebted to his kind, Christian generosity.

Out of fear, Maggie had kept the weekly appointment, after a while it stopped hurting but the humiliation had never lessened. He called her vile names as he pounded into her, everything from a jezebel to an outright whore. And she supposed it wasn't too far from the truth. She was selling herself for her education and an education for her sister.

But she and Gracie had gotten their teaching certification. Grace had been hired to work at the prestigious Garnet School for Young Ladies in Cleveland and Maggie had been sent off to Willet to starve.

There were good things too, like meeting Catherine Elliot. Cat had been sent to the academy by her harried grandparents who wanted to be rid of the responsibly of her. She was smart, wild and she made Maggie laugh. And she too would be home from her position near Chicago for the summer. And there was Grace's announcement that she was engaged to married Phillip Jones, a Cleveland lawyer, who promised to take good care of her and her mother. There had been no mention of Grace's spinster sister in the bargain.

One evening as they sat on the swing on Cat's grandmother's front porch, her friend made a startling confession.

"I lied to you," Cat giggled and grabbed her hands. She leaned in to lower the volume of her voice. "In all those letters I wrote telling you about my school in Chicago, I was lying. I haven't been teaching at all."

She dug in her pocket and looked around to be certain they were not being watched before handing

Maggie a bank book. It was to the Bank of Nebraska, and the total sum in the deposit column said one hundred seventy-five dollars.

"My God, where did you get this kind of money?" Maggie nearly shouted.

Cat pocketed the booklet and shushed her friend. "I've been working in a saloon in Ogallala. I make fifteen dollars a month and all I can win at poker. I get a bed and regular meals. I want you to come with me."

Maggie had noticed that Cat's cheeks had none of the gauntness of her own, and she was wearing a pretty new bonnet.

"I am not going back to trying to pound sums into stupid farm boys' heads when I can just smile and pour cheap whiskey down their dad's throats. I have to be back to work by the first of June. Are you coming?"

Maggie thought about it for a long time, until Deacon Harris had come to Sunday dinner and leered at her over her mother's good china.

She packed her bag that night and threw a pebble at Cat's bedroom window.

"I'll go," she said and waited as her friend began to pack her small case and hurried out to meet her. They caught a train for Ogallala that night and Maggie never looked back.

May 28th 1879

This is either the bravest thing I have ever done or the worst mistake of my life. I feel as if I am standing on the edge of a cliff and I will either fall or fly....

A warm breeze blew in off the prairie and ruffled

the hair Maggie's bonnet didn't cover. She looked out at a world very different from her home. It was a small town; little more than a handful of buildings. Her heart began to race as they got their cases, and Cat led them up the dusty street.

The saloon faced the open prairie only a stone's throw from the massive cattle pens that stretched out to the west of the town.

"Next month," Cat said gesturing to the empty cattle pens. "That will fill up with thousands of heads of cattle being shipped all over the country and the town will fill up with men, starving for a pretty smile and stiff drink."

"I'm nervous," Maggie admitted tightening her grip on her case.

"It's okay. Jackson is going to love you and you're going to love him. He takes good care of us."

Maggie had a sinking feeling in her stomach as she followed her friend, until they stepped in out of the bright afternoon sun. The place was cool and very clean. A well-dressed man was standing at the bar laughing with two young woman dressed in silks and satin. They were the fanciest dresses Maggie had ever seen, and his was the deepest laugh she had ever heard. He turned and gave them a smile and something in Maggie seemed to melt.

He wasn't exactly handsome, but he had a strong face, with a broad nose and dark, flashing eyes and a head completely shaved bald. He looked exotic and so different from anyone Maggie had ever seen in her life. He was dressed head to toe in unrelieved black, that somehow made him look even more striking.

"Well, if it isn't my missing Kitty-Cat?" he said

stepping to meet them. "And she's brought a little friend."

The gaze he fixed on Maggie seemed to break something wide open inside her.

Cat gave him a hug and he kissed her cheek. "I told you that I was coming back, and this is my best friend, Maggie McGregor."

He stepped in front of Maggie and took hold of her shoulders.

She felt an uncomfortable warmth begin to spread through her, heating her face and chest. It spread through her like a barn fire, consuming everything, until it settled in her groin. She fidgeted as he turned his attention to her; her heart was hammering and she got a little lightheaded.

"Hello Maggie. Welcome to the *La Maison Bleue,* the Blue Mansion, I'm the owner and operator, Jackson Bajoliere."

Maggie smiled up and him. "The Blue House. The word mansion is *manoir* in French," she said correcting him. She found herself bracing for some sort of punishment. Maybe he would hit her face or at least put her on a train back to Ohio. Instead he blinked twice and smiled down at her.

"And so it is." He took a step closer and the scent of bay rum and spice filled her senses. "But I've never had anyone know the difference." He leaned in and whispered. "Shall I change the name?"

"I could just keep your secret," she whispered back.

His smile grew wider, he threw back his head and his deep throaty laugh made her knees a little week. This was crazy. She had never had this reaction to a man before and never wanted to have it. This was certainly no time to be swept up in some wild fantasy. He was a saloon owner and a Southern charmer. Not the sort of man a woman set her cap for, even if she was the sort to man-hunt. Maggie wasn't that sort of woman.

"So Miss Maggie. What can I do for you, *mon' cher?*"

"She would like a job."

He gently pinched Cat's cheek between his first two fingers, making her blush, then turned dark unreadable eyes back to Maggie. "Is that right? You want to grace this dull place with your lovely face?" He poured a glass of whiskey.

"For fifteen dollars a month?" Maggie said giving him what she hoped was a beguiling smile. "I certainly do."

He paused and looked her up and down. "Say that again, but this time drop your voice an octave, tip down your chin, give me half the smile, and look up at me through those sooty lashes."

Maggie did as he said. She tipped down her chin, quirked her mouth slightly, and looked up at him through her lashes. "For fifteen dollars a month, I do," she said in a throaty purr. She took the drink from his hand and gave him a salute before sipping the harsh drink daintily.

That smile broadened again. "Oh ma petit, we are going to make a lot of money, you and I."

June 22nd 1879

I have learned to smile and sell drinks to the clientele and dance in my new dresses, but not losing my head around Jackson is another thing all together. I am not sure what I feel for him, but it is powerful. He makes my blood race....

Maggie sat in the dark at the large wooden table in the kitchen in the back of the saloon. She was picking at a piece of fried chicken, when the doors opened and Jackson came in. She felt like a child caught with her hand in the cookie jar.

"Have we not filled you up, *cher?*" he asked pulling out a chair next to her and taking a seat.

She liked to watch him when she was working. The way he smiled, the way he gently dealt with all the girls, even the way he escorted the meanest drunk out the door without losing his patience, impressed her. She had learned her job well. She could talk to strange men, charm them into buying her a very watered down drink, and themselves a strong crude whiskey. She danced and laughed and even played a decent hand of poker. But when he turned his considerable concentration her way, Maggie reverted to a shy, uncomfortable farm girl.

He insisted all the girls call him Jackson. And she loved the sound of his name on her lips.

She smiled. "I'm sorry about the chicken."

He shook his head. "You are welcome to it. Mrs. Bannock says you have a hollow leg, but I think all her good meals have filled your pretty figure out nicely," he said brushing a crumb from her lip.

His finger lingered a moment on her skin and Maggie had a wildest notion to flick her tongue out to taste him. His eyes grew intense and he let his touch slide to her jaw. "God, you are a rare beauty."

She cast her eyes down and Jackson stopped her, tipping her chin to lift her gaze back to his face. "You drop your eyes to no one. Remember that."

She did look into his eyes and took a deep steading breath as his mouth descended to her. The kiss had begun so tenderly, but slowly he moved over her lips, playing them gently apart until Maggie opened to him. He kissed her soundly brushing her tongue and sending a thrill down her spine. He pulled her tightly against him and Maggie was suddenly aware of how big he was, how hard his muscles were under the fine cotton shirt he wore and how warm his arms felt as they slipped around her.

Her heart was slamming against her ribs, and her blood hammered in her ears. She leaned into his touch relishing the feel of his strength, the power in his body. Her nerves began to hum with excitement. This was completely foreign to her. So far from anything she had imagined or even experienced at the hands of the deacon. This made her breath catch in her throat.

He stopped and began to push her away. "I think we better say good night, Miss Maggie. Or I'm liable to do something you might regret."

Maggie caught his arm before he pulled away. "I won't regret anything," she said breathlessly.

"You know what you're fooling with, girl?" he asked.

"Yes. No. I'm not sure but I want... something... more." She felt like a fool but she couldn't seem to stop herself. She wanted his kisses, his touch... and something else.

Jackson studied her in the dim kitchen light and took her hand. "Come, *cher*."

He led her up the back stairs to the second floor, passed the room where the girls slept, and then up another narrow set of stairs. His private rooms were tucked up in the dormered roof of the saloon. She found a large room with a worn sofa and a roll top desk. On the far side of the room was a large ornate metal bed covered with quilts and thick pillows.

She was in his room. Her heart was pounding so hard she thought she might faint. She had given herself to a man she hated; now she wanted to give herself to one she wanted. And oh, how she wanted him. She turned and stepped closer, tipping her face up to him.

He drew her to him and kissed her hard, parting her lips and claiming her mouth with a commanding possession until she caught on to his rhythm and began to kiss him back. The play of her tongue on his made him growl, a deep sound that seemed to vibrate through her whole body. His hands moved up her body crushing her to him and traveling over her curves. He cupped her breast and Maggie gasped, the warmth of his hand through the layers of her chemise and dress seemed to sear her skin. Her nipples pebbled and he drew his thumb over one, moaning softly against the sensitive skin of her neck. He kissed and tasted her throat and down to her collarbone.

Her dress was low and his kisses trailed over her exposed décolletage. He pressed up on the underside of her breast and it slipped from the cover of her dress. He took the rosy nipple into his mouth, sucking it gently at first, then harder, until it was Maggie who groaned.

Maggie knew what he wanted and how to give him what he commanded. She turned herself and lifted her skirts. She drew down her bloomers and began to bend over the side of the desk presenting him with her naked buttocks. She spread her legs and prepared to be mounted.

"*Cher*, this is a lovely view, I'll grant you, but what are you doing?" he asked turning her back to face him again.

"I thought you wanted to..." the words trailed off.

"I want you desperately. See." He took her hand and pressed it to the hard bulge at his crotch. "I'm harder than a rail spike, but I'm still puzzled by what you think you're doing bending over my desk." His voice ran over her like warm honey.

"I thought..."

"You thought I'd take you like that, mount you like a horse." He took her hand and led her to the side of his bed. She hadn't thought about lying down, or even how a man and woman might do it that way.

"There is more to sex than a man slaking his lust on you, my petit. There is the sharing of heart and souls. There is the sharing of secrets." Again he pressed her hand to his crotch. "See how you make me hard. I'm burning to taste your beautiful body to spread your lovely legs. But I want more, my belle, I want to make love to you. So we share our secrets and then we share our bodies."

"I have no secrets," she lied.

"Everyone has secrets." He slipped the narrow strap of her dress off one shoulder. "I'll begin."

He turned her slightly and began to undo the row of small buttons down her back. "I was born in New Orleans, Louisiana. My mother's name was Gabriella Bajoliere. She was an Octoroon, a Creole courtesan."

"A what?" she said leaning back to feel his touch

19

against her bare back. His hands spread out over her ribs, helping her slide her dress from her arms. Her breasts were exposed but she concentrated on his deep melodic voice.

"She was a Madame, and she ran a fine house in Storyville, Louisiana. My Pere was one of her wealthy clients. And her *mamere*, my grandmother was born a slave."

Maggie stepped from her dress and stood for a moment in the moonlight streaming through the window. His gaze ran over her and he smiled. "My God, but you are breathtakingly beautiful. Share your secrets with me."

Maggie looked up at him and her voice came softly at first. "I am no virgin."

"Not because you wanted to give it away?" He unbuttoned his shirt and pulling it from the waist of his pants. "You were wronged by a heartless man."

Her gaze fell on the broad, bulging muscles of his chest. He was a big man and his muscles were thick and strong.

"The deacon of our church. He was the one who bent me over his desk and took my flower. I did it once a week for two years as we attended his school for teachers."

"Cur. God must hate such men." He took her hands and moved them to the buttons of his pants. "I will not force you, Maggie. If you want me to love you, to show you what can be between a man and woman, you must take me."

She smiled at that, and undid the buttons. She pushed his trousers over his hips and ran her hands over the smooth, hard muscles of his hips. A bit lower his engorged manhood appeared. She paused, and swallowed hard. He was so big, much bigger than Deacon Harris. It stood out from a thatch of black hair that curled in the apex of his heavily corded thighs. He lowered his trousers to the floor and sat on the bed to remove his leather cowboy boots.

"Your preacher was unkind and ungenerous. I won't do that to you, *cher*."

When his clothes were gone, he took her hands and gently guided her to the edge of the mattress.

"Teach me," she said and sat next to him.

Maggie followed his lead, returning his kisses and letting her hands learn the angles and curves of his body. Now when he guided her fingers to his crotch, her hand filled with heated flesh. He was hard as living stone.

"You feel like you're throbbing."

"I can make you throb too, *cher*," he whispered, and he kissed her breast, licking her nipples and drawing them in and out of his hot mouth. As he did this, one hand began to knead the soft flesh of her other breast and his other hand climbed her thigh. His fingers brushed into her pubic curls. He urged her legs apart and his fingers slid into the folds of her flesh. She could feel that her body had become wet and hot. Her nerve endings jumped and she twitched under his touch.

"Relax, ma belle. Let me show you."

She took a deep breath and relaxed as he kissed her again. As hard and demanding as his mouth was his hand and fingers were gentle and probing. He began to stroke her flesh and she felt a tightness start. He skillfully played her genitals, stroking, delving deeper, and spreading the wetness over her folded skin. He found the bud of her desire. Maggie bucked against his hand, closing her legs.

The tension built as he stroked the source of her pleasure. His fingers moved faster and he took her nipple in his mouth again. He suckled her deep and slid his finger deeper, stoking broader.

Maggie writhed on the bed, gripping the quilt in both fists as this tremendous pressure build in her body. Her hips began to pump against his hand. He released her breast and leaned back to watch her pleasure.

"Let go, *cher*. Let it take you. Let it drive you."

His hand was now pumping her surface, and diving deep into her forbidden folds.

Suddenly, she felt as if she had burst wide open. She arched her back and let out a small scream of joy as she experienced her first orgasm.

He sat quietly stocking her heated skin and cooing in her ear as she seemed to float back down to earth back to the world of his bed, his mouth, his hands. He moved closer and she felt his hard erection probe her hip. She knew he wanted her, wanted to bury himself in her. But he held back.

She took his dick in her hands but he pulled away.

"Not yet, my petit. There is more for you to learn." He came over her, starting to kiss her mouth and then moving down her neck and over her taut breasts. He kissed her belly and Maggie found herself bracing her hands against his broad shoulders. He kissed lower over her navel and down until his lips met the curls of her Venus mound.

"Oh Jackson," she sighed as his mouth found the

wet folds of her skin. His tongue found the place his fingers had taught to want. He licked and suckled, delving deeply until that glorious pressure began to build again. He blew on her heated skin and kissed her deeply. This time she knew what to expect but as his tongue began to flick wildly over her bud she exploded. He ran his tongue into her and Maggie bucked against his mouth. She ran her hands over this slick smooth head and held him to her.

His face was wet with her cum as he parted her legs and slid into her with one hard thrust. He pumped her body hard. Maggie caught his rhythm and met each hard thrust with a subtle tilt of her pelvis.

"Yes, Jackson!" she cried as he took her harder, deeper.

She hadn't thought that anything could feel better than his fingers, his mouth had felt, but the fullness of his long, hard dick was a glory she could not have imagined possible. He rode her hard, until she came again and he drove into her in his own release.

She lay at his side as Jackson gently toyed with her body. He touched, kissed, stroked her body, keeping her aroused while he let her rest from their play.

"You see what you can do? See what we were built to share. Your preacher was a fool to take without giving. It's the sharing of pleasure that makes it so wonderful."

"You're wonderful," she breathed. "I felt like I was flying."

"My angel," he said kissing her deeply.

"Is this real?" she asked.

He gathered her closer.

Maggie snuggled closer and her hands began to

search him again.

"No, my petit. You have learned enough tonight. Sleep and dream." He pulled her close and they fell deeply asleep.

July 23rd, 1879

My skin is still warm from his touch, my heart still full from his attention. I will never be the same.

For the next month Maggie lived to be with Jackson, every moment she could wrap herself around his perfect body, to open herself body and soul, she did it. She was sore and tired and happier than she could remember feeling. Jackson smiled and caressed her when he walked past her. They were sharing a secret, a passion that was only their own.

The men from the King Ranch outside of town had come into town with nearly two thousand head of cattle that would be sold in the market to the meat packers of Chicago or the US Army and shipped out. They had worked hard days. At night, they were ready to blow off a little steam.

Maggie was dealing cards at a table for Race King and four of his cowboys and pouring the gentlemen from the bar's most expensive bottle of bourbon. Race, a handsome older man with a voice even deeper than Jackson's was trying to charm her into helping him cheat.

"You're going to get me into trouble, Mr. King."

"I would sooner die a thousand deaths, pretty lady."

Jackson gave her a wink and kept the whiskey

flowing. When the evening was coming to a close, Race asked Maggie to join him in his room upstairs but didn't take her rejection hard. In fact, he pressed a coin into her hand and a kiss on her cheek before taking himself up the stairs alone. Maggie stared down at the four dollar piece.

"Imagine what he would have given you to go upstairs with him," Opal said with a wink.

Jackson waited until the others had gone home or off to bed. Then he smiled and took Maggie's hand, leading her up the stairs to his room.

Nothing was said as they hurriedly stripped off their clothes. His hard body was a marvel to her, so incredibly beautiful. He kissed her deeply, and moved his hands over her skin setting fire to her nerve endings. She tossed back her head and reveled in the thrill of his touch. His dick grew hard against her.

"You make me so happy," she said, running her hands over his pectorals and down over the muscles of his stomach.

"My pleasure, *cher*," he purred, raining kissed down over her breasts.

"I want to pleasure you," she said, careful to cover the quiver of nervousness in her voice. "I want you to feel the way I did."

"Believe me. You make me feel incredible." He punctuated his comment by taking the tip of one pink nipple into his mouth.

Maggie groaned and arched her back to give him more access to her, then caught herself. "No. I want to learn to pleasure you. To make you feel the things you made me feel. I know you have probably been having…"

"Sex," he supplied.

"… for a long time."

"Since I was fourteen. Celestina was a pretty little Creole strumpet who worked for my mother. She was probably only sixteen or seventeen then, but she was such a woman and a wonderful teacher."

"I want to be that kind of woman, to be able to take control of you the way you did me, to make you quiver and…"

"Beg?" he said, his lips pressed to the sensitive flesh of her nipple.

"Yes. I want you to beg for the things you gave me."

He laughed and took her shoulders in his hands. 'You are always so serious about these things. It's sex, *cher*. It is bodies and heat and connections, not a lesson to be learned."

"I was a teacher once, everything is a lesson. Teach me, Jackson." She started to wrap her legs around his waist and Jackson stopped her.

"If you want to learn to pleasure a man, then you must think about his body."

Maggie pulled away and stood ready to learn. "Your perfect body."

He cupped her cheek. "Thank you, *Précieux*. But you have to learn what makes it work, what makes it want."

He pointed to his lips. "Here."

His nipples. "Here."

She slid her hand down wrapping her hand around his stiff shaft.

"Here," she said.

"Absolutely, and here." He guided her hand back

to cup his testicles.

She rolled them in her hand and he groaned. "There are a few lesser places that you can touch or kiss."

She thought about herself, the places he had concentrated on and kissed his mouth hard, then moved to the spot behind his ear. She drew her teeth down the tendon of his neck and noted that he shivered. She trailed her tongue over his collar bone and into the hollow at the base of his throat.

"You are a quick study."

She traced kisses down his chest and over the rise of his left pectoral. She took his dark pap between her lips, kissing, licking and then sucking it greedily into her mouth. It felt good when he groaned and cupped the back of her neck with his strong hands. She lavished attention on the nipple and began to move to the other when his husky voice stopped her.

"Always take your time, *cher*. Hold the moment as long as you can and you'll build the pleasure."

She did as he instructed, taking her time, loving him with her mouth, slowly adding her fingers, touching, teasing stroking his skin until he shivered under her fondling. Her slender fingers slid over his abdomen and down the tight V that led to his swollen dick. She curled one hand around the thick shaft and with the other she cupped his heavy balls.

He purred deeply, a rumble in his chest that set a fire in the pit of her stomach. She wanted him, but more importantly she wanted him to want her, to need her as much as she needed him. He had given her so much, a life really. And she would give him this, her body, her heart, her will, anything he asked for.

She would do her best to make him feel like a king.

She fondled him, gently, slowly until he was hard as a rock, shaking with desire and moaning her name.

"Ma petit, you are killing me."

"I don't want that," she purred and began to follow her fingers with kisses. She ran her tongue around the dark nipple then lower over his hard-muscled stomach, he watched her slowly lower herself in front of him. She was eye level with his engorged penis, and suddenly nervous about what she intended to do.

He reached down cupping her cheek. "You don't have to do this."

"I want to," she took a deep breath and licked her lips.

"Kiss me."

She kissed the tip of his penis.

He sighed. "Take your time. Get to know the feel of it, the shape. There is no more matter of pride on a man's body like this. Love it and he will love you. It will make a man do foolish things. The head is so sensitive. The *vaisseau sanguin* under the shaft runs like a river of fire."

She did take her time, touching, caressing, fondling him. It was so hard, but so delicate. It was suddenly kind of funny. She had feared going to the Deacon's office. The thought of his pathetically tiny dick had given her nightmares. But here she was faced with a man, a bull of a man, and there was no fear.

She kissed him again, then opened her mouth and took the tip into her mouth. He filled her mouth and she tensed.

"Relax," he said. "You have control. Don't hold your breath."

His deep voice seemed to penetrate her, and she did relax, opening her mouth wider. She took him deeper, expecting to gag on the bulk of him. She didn't. She pulled him out slightly and then took him back. She slowly worked him in and out of her mouth. Soon she had caught a rhythm, driving him until he could no longer talk. He gripped the post of the bed and groaned like a madman.

Suddenly he stopped, tensed and pushed her away but not before the white hot stream of seed shot from him, landing on her naked breasts.

He leaned heavily into the post. His breath was heavy and ragged. "I am sorry, *petit.*"

She stood, smiling. "I'll remember to be more careful the next time."

He breathed heavily but took a thick towel from his wash stand. He rubbed the soft rag on her skin, washing away the evidence of his passion. "You are such a quick study."

"I want to learn everything."

"I feel alive and free. I've been so afraid of… everything, and now…" She stepped close, pressing her body to his and wriggled her body against his. He wrapped his strong arms around her and she felt small and fragile but not weak. "I will never be weak again."

"Ah, ma petit, you are a goddess. My goddess."

Again she began to play with his body, touching and teasing until she had roused his passions again. When he was hard and ready for her, Maggie wrapped her legs around him. Jackson cupped her round bottom and lifted her. With a tilt of her hips she slid onto his engorged manhood. She was wet with desire, the tender flesh of her vagina throbbed with need.

"Do that," he said tightly as she tilted her hips back and forth, pulled away and then taking him deeply into her again.

"Does that feel good?" she cooed.

"My goddess." He pumped into her, driving into her flesh.

Maggie threw back her head, her dark hair swinging around them as she rode him, dragging his hard erection over her needy flesh, again and again, harder, faster until her back was against the hard post. He pushed into her hard tipping her into the place of madness.

He held her tighter and hammered into her in his own climax.

Together they fell onto his bed, Exhausted and happy, she slept in his arms.

August 29th 1879

I have changed so completely. I want nothing more than to spend the rest of my life here, with this man, I'm stronger but I am more than that, I'm not going to let anyone have control of me again....

Maggie sat in the back of the saloon shuffling her cards and watching Jackson pace the floor, shouting at his partner, Billy Pardue. He was worried and angry enough that most of what he said was a strange mix of English, French, spoken in his familiar Cajun dialect. She had never seen him this upset. Occasionally, he would pour a drink and glance her way. He smiled as if to reassure her that it wasn't her, he was furious with. She knew that and she knew who he was angry at.

Gus Friday.

The flashy Texan had opened a saloon, The Bull, only three doors down from *La Maison Bleue*. From the time he had opened the doors, Jackson had been losing money.

Jackson called him a pig, a goat, and if she understood his angry Cajun, a grey monkey. Billy was speechless after an hour of his friend's hot temper. Jackson needed to calm down.

Maggie poured some of the good bourbon and took it to him. "Before you drag any more animals into this, tell me what it going on and how I can help."

He took the drink and patted her cheek. "Ah babe, there is nothing anyone can do. He has drink, food and a Faro dealer. Now, he is keeping a stable of girls in those filthy cribs out back of his building. Men are standing three deep at his bar and this place as an eglise."

Maggie took a seat at the empty table near the bar and snickered softly. "No one will mistake this place for a church. We just need a plan to bring the men back. Have you thought about having girls here?"

He shrugged a wide shoulder. "I have but getting good girls is not easy. I would have to bring them in from out of town. The pickings here are too slim."

"What about us?" Callie Porter said. She was a plump little farm girl from Virginia.

"You're not prostitute. There is a big difference, between selling beer and selling your pretty tails."

Callie and her close friend Edna Pinks passed a look.

"What is it?" Maggie asked.

Edna sighed. "I have done that sort of thing."

"Me too," Callie said.

"And me," Opal Grainger piped up.

"Callie and me had to make money to get out here. It wasn't as hard as fightin' off my six-fingered cousins," she said with a shrug.

"I worked in a house in Chicago and wanted a rest."

"Would you work for Jackson?" Maggie asked.

The women passed a look around and Edna smiled. "How much do we get paid for it?"

Maggie looked at Jackson and raised her brows.

He sighed. "And additional two dollars a month."

"Ten?" Edna countered.

Jackson muttered. "Oo ye yi,"

"Better hurt than broke." Maggie pointed out.

"Who's side are you on?" he asked pinching her cheek between his first too fingers and smiling. "Five."

"Done!" Edna said.

"But you must be the best, no drunkenness and no swearing. You must be proper ladies. No one will pay top rate for girls who act low down," he insisted.

Maggie glanced at Cat who was worrying her lower lip between her teeth. Maggie took her sleeve and led her away. "What's wrong, honey?"

"I don't think I can do this, Maggie," she said softly.

"Jackson won't make you do anything you don't want to. He'll understand."

"What about you?" Cat asked. "I know you're sleeping with Jackson. Can you do this?"

Maggie surprised herself by pausing. Could she do it, give herself to another man, let another man touch her like Jackson did? She didn't think so. He was her lover, her rock in this strange place.

"No," she said finally and gave her friend a reassuring hug. "I can't do that either."

Jackson came to them and chucked Catherine's cheek. "Will you stay and continue to work for me, with this kind of business going on?"

"If I can," Cat said. "I can still serve drinks and deal cards."

"Of course, *Ma Chat*! I cannot lose such a beauty."

October 10th 1879

The changes here are amazing. Word about Jackson's beautiful girls was spreading through Ogallala, faster than a prairie fire. The girls' reputations for beauty, grace and skills were becoming legend. My love for Jackson grows stronger each day, and I do what I can to help him....

Maggie wasn't sure when she had taken over the business of the brothel. It had happened slowly, a lesson in the finer points of pouring a drink. Then a lesson in diction and deportment that would have reduced the teachers at Miss Garnet's School for Young Ladies to fits of apoplexy. She thought about her mother and the others at First Baptist Church, their phony piety and pompous airs. They would have turned up their noses and sniffed at the thought of these women comporting themselves as ladies. But they learned, they could brew a perfect pot of tea, mix a hot toddy, brush a man's jacket and polish his boots. They could play the piano, sing and dance all the most popular dances. And most important, to make each client feel like he is the most important person in the world, for the evening they were in their company.

The average soiled dove was hired by the hour, a fifty pence piece, half a dollar for a poke that was quick and too often, dirty. But Jackson's girls worked by completely different criteria. Two dollars for the evening, four for the night was an exorbitant amount, but, remarkably, the expensive nature of the cattleman tastes had fuel the competition for Jackson's girls. It stroked the egos of egoistical men and Jackson was happy to take their money for it.

For the girls, doing a good job, making them men's fantasies come true had become an economic boon. The original pay of twenty dollars a month, more than even a good cowboy made, renegotiated to be half the fee of each after hour job. Most of the girls were making more than thirty dollars, and that from working less than fifteen days a month. A truly ambitious girl could make even more. Opal was making nearly fifty dollars a month. Most of the girls had regulars, men who paid even more for the privilege of picking and choosing their time with the girls.

Maggie managed their time, arranged their clients and handled the money. She had a good head for figures and didn't mind the extra job.

Her days were filled with caring for her girls and her nights with caring for Jackson.

Saturdays were the liveliest night. She would dance and deal poker for the evening, talking the men into a night with Callie or Opal and keeping the place busy and earning money. Jackson played the perfect host, keeping the conversations going, the booze flowing and the clients happy. Everyone was happy but Maggie noticed a change in Catherine Elliot.

Her usually happy, smiling friend had turned quiet and sullen. She did her job, flirting, dancing and pouring drinks, but she did it without her usual bright smile and giddy laugh. Maggie found her alone in the kitchen long before the others woke. She was staring into a cup of coffee.

Maggie poured herself a cup and sat opposite her. "Are you all right?"

Cat swept a tear from her cheek and looked up, a determined but artificial smile on her face. "I'm doing great."

"Are you certain?"

Her face twisted slightly and tears filled her eyes. "No. I've made a terrible mistake."

"What? What did you do?" Maggie slid her chair closer to her friend.

"Jackson is going to be so angry at me," she sobbed.

"No." Maggie said. "Jackson loves you. He would never be angry at you. Why would you think that?"

Cat wiped at her tears. Maggie shook out a lace handkerchief and blotted her flushed cheeks.

"Do you know Harvey Tellmen?"

"The Faro dealer over at The Bull. I've seen him."

"He and I . . . I thought we were going to get married. He wanted to buy a ranch and raise cattle and kids. I love him so much. We've been having sex for over a month."

Maggie didn't understand. "That sounds lovely. A house and a family."

But she only cried harder, hiccupping loudly. Her nose was a bright red and her eyes were swollen and red. "He left town with Binnie Tucker, one of the girls that works for Gus."

Maggie gave her a hug. Cat sobbed for a long time and Maggie softly cried with her. Her friend was devastated and there was nothing she could do to help her. She was in pain and all Maggie could do was hold her and let her cry.

She didn't want to think about the kind of hurt Cat was feeling. For a moment she let herself think what she would do if Jackson pulled up stakes and moved on without her. She would be the one weeping. She wasn't sure what she would do without Jackson, and she wasn't sure she liked that.

Catherine was mumbling about losing everything, dying alone and having no one that cared about her.

Maggie had learned a long time ago not to rely on anyone for her needs. Even the people she loved, her mother, her sister Grace had taken care of themselves and not bothered to notice that Maggie had been starving and lonely and hurting.

"Listen to me," Maggie said brushing Cat's pale hair from her face. "I love you. You're my family. I will never let you be alone. Do you hear me?"

Cat sniffled but nodded her head. "What if I'm pregnant?"

That was something she had thought about herself. "Then we'll have a baby. You and me, and Jackson and Billy and Opal. We're your family and you're ours. We'll take care of you."

Her friend smiled weakly, but she had stopped crying and only hiccupped a time or two. "Thank you."

Maggie put a pot of water on the stove and put tea in a porcelain pot. In a few minutes the rich smell of tea filled the kitchen.

When Maggie came back with two cups of tea and a bowl of sugar, Cat only sighed. "Do you miss home?"

"I miss Grace and I wish I had brought my father's ledgers. It was the only thing he ever wrote other than a letter he sent me from Chicago once."

"Your dad was a nice man."

"I miss him, but no, I don't miss New Philadelphia. I'm happy where I am."

"Jackson is your lover, isn't he?"

Maggie started to deny it but she stopped herself. "Yes."

"Are you going to marry him?"

"We've never talked about that."

"Isn't it what you want?" Cat asked.

Maggie thought about it as she ushered her friend to bed and then crawled in next to Jackson's warm sleeping body. Did she want to be a wife or a mother? She had never given that much thought to being married. She had spent so much time trying to get an education, to get a teaching position, to get a life that she hadn't thought about what might come next.

Jackson rolled toward her and put a big strong arm over her.

"I love you," she whispered and Jackson stirred again, pulling her closer.

She snuggled in closer, planting a kiss on his neck and gliding her fingertips over the ripple of muscles over his stomach. Maggie let her fingers drift lower until she brushed the tightly curled hair that crowned his penis. She threaded her fingers into the thick thatch of hair and found the treasure she wanted.

He was still asleep as she took his flaccid member into her hand. She gently massaged the base of his shaft, slowly bringing it to life. She cupped his scrotum and massaged them between her fingers. She pressed her mouth to his.

Jackson moaned in his sleep, gathering Maggie close and kissing her deeply.

"Do you want to wake up and play?" she purred into his ear.

"Always," he kissed his way down her limbs rousing her body as she had his. He licked and suckled her breasts, while fondling the lush bud of her clitoris, until Maggie threw back her head, begging him to release her.

And Maggie stoked his hardened dick until it throbbed against her hand.

Finally she spread her legs and welcomed him into her. A hard thrust and she tightened her flesh around him. Again and again he pumped into her, deeper and harder until she groaned his name and clung to him to as she climaxed.

He hammered into her and exploded in his own massive finish.

They lay, still joined as one, panting and sweating, their hearts pounding against their ribs. After a while they peeled themselves apart but didn't let go. Maggie needed his arms, his strength, as her mind drifted to her friend probably crying herself to sleep below stairs. It broke her heart.

It was so damned unfair that a man could come and go so easily through this life, taking what he wanted, hurt who he wished, and a woman was still held to the archaic notion she was nothing more than

an appendage in a man's life. Catherine was an intelligent, caring woman paying the price for trusting a man who didn't deserve her love or her trust.

"What's wrong, *cher?*" Jackson asked brushing threads of damp hair from her face.

Maggie sighed and pulled him closer. "I'm afraid," she admitted softly.

"Afraid? Of what," he asked, pulling her head down to his shoulder.

She was being ridiculous. She wasn't Cat. She was lying in the arms of the man she loved. She was safe.

But how safe?

If Jackson tired of her, or if he simply changed his mind about the whole thing, she would be Cat. She would be just as broken and just as lost.

She curled next to his chest where she could hear the strong reassuring pound of his heart against her cheek. She did that, she made his heart pound and his dick swell and his body throb. But couldn't any woman do that?

"Cat has been sleeping with Harvey Tellman."

Jackson leaned back and looked into her face. "I heard he just left town with Skinny Binnie."

"He did, and Cat is heartbroken."

"What was she doing messin' with that *couyon*."

She furrowed her brow. "I don't know that word."

"Ignorant ass… more or less. Why was she messing around with him?"

"She wasn't messing around. She was in love with him. She thought he was going to marry her, make a home with her. Now, she is alone and hurting. I don't know what to do for her."

He pulled her against his chest. "There is nothing we can do but love her and let her know that she has a home with us. I wonder if he taught her to deal Faro?"

Maggie wasn't sure she heard him. "Faro? Is that all you can think about? Getting a faro dealer out of the deal?"

"No! Of course, not. I was thinking about Cat and her future. She can make a lot of money dealing Faro."

Maggie pushed off him and stepped out of bed. She pulled the blanket off him and wound it around herself.

"Where are you going, *cher?*"

"To my bed. I need to be alone to think."

He leaned back on his down pillow and gave her a seductive smile. "Your bed might be cold, Maggie."

She leaned in a kissed him, but turned and went to her room. She could hear Cat crying through her closed door and the sound of grunts as Edna was entertaining the foreman from the King Ranch. She turned the corner in the hallway and ran right into Race King.

"Well, Miss Maggie," he said his smooth deep voice washing over her. He was at least two decades older than her, but he was big and solid and smelled like leather and wood smoke. He held her a moment or two in his arms then glanced down at the creamy curve of her breast and smiled.

She should have been shocked, horrified that she was naked, alone and vulnerable with a stranger. But she didn't feel those things. He looked at her with desire, a hunger she had the power to relieve.

She felt powerful.

"Hello, Mr. King," she said softly. "I beg your pardon."

He smiled. "I was going to visit Callie but if you--"

"No, I'm not entertaining."

He tipped his hat and released her. "If you decide

to begin, I would pay small fortune for the honor of your company."

She turned and hurried to her room, flipping the lock and slid into her bed.

At noon, Jackson came down the stairs and found the girls gathered around Catherine. They had discussed how horrible Harvey was and how cruel he was, and how stupid he was for taking Skinny Binnie with him. They all cried and promised to do anything in their power to help.

Jackson brought her a glass of his good bourbon and sat next to her holding his hand. "If you want to take a day or two, *cheri*. We all understand."

"No," Cat said and downed the bourbon in one quick gulp. She coughed a little but stood up. "I want to dance. Maggie can you play me something lively? Come on, Lucas." She grabbed Luke Stewart's hands and led him to the open part of the floor. "Dance with me."

They danced to a reel and a polka and then a waltz, while Maggie played and the others joined in. Jackson danced with Edna, then Callie and finally convinced Opal to take over the piano and he twirled Maggie around the hardwood floor. Their skirts flew up and their shoes taped out a load tattoo as the women flew from one man to the next. Maggie finished the dance with Race King, who bowed gallantly. Everyone hurried to the bar for a drink and for the rest of the night they forgot about their cares.

Cat surprised Maggie by deciding to spend the night with Luke for a hefty fee.

Maggie found her way back to Jackson's bedroom

and his waiting arms.

December 20th 1879

The weather is turning colder but winter is not the only drastic change here....

Early in the winter, Billy came down with a fever that left him weak in the lungs and Jackson suggested he avoid the long, blistering Nebraska winter and head back to New Orleans. His old friend put up a fight, pointing out that Jackson had no idea how to handle the books or place the orders. Maggie was surprised to find out how much Billy did for the saloon. He was the brains behind the thriving business, while Jackson was the charming face of *Le Maison Bleue*. She asked Billy if she could take over for him. He agreed to sit down and walk her through the job of business accountant.

Maggie had a very good head for business. She handled the bills and pay roll. She managed the payments to suppliers. She even handled the sizable amounts sent every month to Jackson's mother, Mrs. Bajoliere in the Garden District of New Orleans. The first bank draft she sent to the woman, she included a brief hand written note. Her hand shook slightly as she penned the personal message.

Dear Mrs. Bajoliere,

My name is Maggie and I am taking over the books for Billy Pardue while he returns home to care for himself. I am thrilled to be working for a man as fine as your son, Jackson. He is held in high esteem by all of us here at the

La Maison Bleue. I understand that it was commonplace for you to contact Billy when any need arose. Please feel free to also call upon me in the future.

If you need anything at all contact me at La Maison Bleue. I am at your disposal.

Sincerely,
M. McGregor

Maggie also took care of the girls, seeing them outfitted in the latest fashions. She also took a lot of pride in taking the girls out to show them off. They never went anywhere that they were not dressed to the nines with perfectly fitted and maintained clothes and perfectly coifed hair. They also attended church every Sunday morning, each girl wearing pristine white gloves and carrying new Bibles. Maggie gave them each a dollar to add to the collection plate.

The men were beginning to come to the saloon days in advance to get evenings with their favorite girl. Jackson credited Maggie with the sudden spike in attention and the steady windfall of money. He gave her a raise.

She was now making thirty dollars a month and she kept 100% her poker winnings.

March 1st 1880

Jackson says he is proud of me for all the hard work I have been doing here. I would move heaven and earth for him. We have each other. But in the end, I wonder how much I really have and how much I am merely hoping for. I find myself wishing for something real….

Maggie was spending as much time staring out the window at the quickly growing grass of the open prairie as she was dealing cards to the four men sitting across the round table from her. There was so much about her life that had changed, but not her view. There was not much difference between the vast Nebraska sky and the open vista she had grown up seeing every day. Race King tapped his cards to indicate he wanted two new cards. Maggie missed the gesture entirely.

"Where is your head girl?" he asked taking two cards from the deck in her hand.

"I'm sorry Mr. King, I was wool gathering."

"You were wandering out there somewhere." He nodded to the window. "What are you hoping to see?"

"Nothing really." She dealt cards to Frank Carlson, Harry Boater and the greasy man who called himself Reverend Perch. "How far west have you traveled?"

"I took five hundred head of steer to Camp Collins a few summers back."

"Colorado?" she asked, leaning forward. "I hear it's beautiful."

King gathered his hand and tapped her cards to remind her of her game. She looked at the two aces in her hand, and drew three cards. She schooled her face not to show her excitement.

"It was the prettiest country I've ever seen. Took my breath clean away, sorta like you, Maggie dear."

"Are we talking or playing poker?" the traveling minister grumbled into his glass of cheap whiskey.

"You in an all fired hurry to lose your last handful of coins, parson?" Harry Boater laughed.

"I ain't gonna lose," Perch said and wiped his nose on his sleeve.

"Then I'll see your bet and raise you fifty saw-bucks." King put a fist full of crisp bills on the table and leaned back in his chair.

Maggie smiled. Leaning back was Race's tell. He was bluffing and he had just put a small fortune on the table.

"I'm out." Harry said dropping his pair of threes on the table.

Frank studied his and then laughed. "Me too." His handful of unrelated cards joined the discards.

The turn came to the Reverend. He had started to sweat, there was a small tremble in his right hand and he gulped a mouthful of whiskey as though he had just crawled through a desert on his hands and knees. He wiped at his mouth. He believed in his hand but not enough to pounce on the pot. And he was low on funds. Maggie had watched him pick through a small coin bag before putting down his ante for the hand.

"Come on, padre," Race prodded.

"I've got a tent, donated by one of the faithful. It's nearly brand new, not so much as a patch on it. It cost more than fifty dollars. It'll cover my bet."

Race and Maggie shared a look and the cowboy lifted a shoulder. "It's fine by me, if it's fine by the lady."

Perch made a derisive sound. "Lady? She ain't no lady."

King started to come out of his chair and Maggie stopped him with a hand to his sleeve.

"I'm fine with the bet, Mr. King." She took fifty dollars out of the stack of money she had been growing

45

all afternoon. "I call."

Perch put out his three tens and grinned at Race King. "Beat that."

Race shook his head. "Got me beat." He tossed down his pair of Jacks.

The grimy preacher started to reach for the cash, when Maggie smacked his hand. "Ah-ah. Full house, aces over queens."

She fanned the cards out and the minister sunk into his chair and put his hands on his head.

Maggie giggled as she gathered the cash in a tidy pile and couldn't stop the smile. She would give Jackson half of the take but she had just earned herself thirty dollars and apparently, a revival tent.

The old minister turned a dark shade of red and fumbled to make a noise somewhere between a grunt and a shout. Then suddenly Reverend Perch found his voice. "You bitch."

"Now Perch," Jackson said, stepping away from the bar. "You lost the hand fair and square."

"She's a cheating viper," the man shouted.

A string of evil words continued to spew from the man as Jackson walked to the table with a bottle of the cheap whiskey in his hand. "Have a drink and cool off."

"Filthy whore," Perch roared.

He came up with a gun in his hand and Maggie felt her chest tighten as the barrel wavered in front of her face. A second before the gun spat fire at her, it shot upward, the bullet hitting the ceiling and sending shards of wood raining down on her.

It wasn't Jackson who had saved her life, but Race King who gripped the Reverend's wrist. He hit Perch so hard in the face that he crumbled to the floor. Jackson had backed away. She stared at him, as another man stepped up to be her hero.

"Take this piece of shit to the sheriff." King barked at two of his ranch hands and threw the reverend toward the door.

"Go see if that fool did any damage upstairs," Jackson shouted at Bud the bartender.

It was King again that came to Maggie.

"Thank you, Mr. King," Maggie said softly.

He swept his hat from his head and he knelt by Maggie's chair. "Are you okay, darlin'?"

She took the hand he offered. "I'm fine. Just a little shaken up. I'll be okay."

"Get me a glass of whiskey. The good stuff, not that rotgut you served Perch," King shouted at Jackson.

Old Barnes, one of the regulars brought him a glass and Race passed it to her. She realized her hand was shaking. He stopped and took her hand in his. "I'm sorry Maggie. I should have stopped him sooner."

Maggie wrapped her other hand around his and leaned against his strength. "No, you were wonderful. You saved my life. Thank you." He helped her from her chair and escorted her to the stairs where she stopped him. "I'll be fine."

Jackson started to follow her and she suddenly didn't want him to follow. She didn't need his comfort and she didn't want his belated concern.

"I'll be fine," she said stopping him as well. "I just need to rest."

Jackson looked confused, then slightly embarrassed. "I'm sorry," he said softly, and Maggie cupped his cheek.

She didn't go up the third floor to Jackson's bedroom but stopped at the second floor room that she and Cat had been assigned months ago. She stretched out on the bed and tried to close her eyes. It was nearly impossible with all the noise and activity going on down stairs. But eventually the fear and tension overtook her and she dropped off into an uneasy sleep.

In her dreams, she was back in that chair, the cool surface of her cards in her hand. Perch's hateful glare bore into her. She could see Jackson in the background laughing and chatting with strangers. This time the gun barked and the smoke and fire it spewed burned into her face. She couldn't breathe, her chest tightened and she fell to the floor. The last thing she saw was Race King's face staring down at her.

She sat up and wiped the sweat from her face. After a few moments to collect herself, she did her best to straighten her dress and hair before descending the steps to join the others. Jackson took her arm and led her to the bar like a returning hero.

"How are you feeling, Maggie?" he asked. "Buddy, get Miss Maggie a glass of sherry."

"I'm fine," she assured them all.

"A round on the house to celebrate our Maggie." Jackson said lifting his own glass of whiskey.

The large crowd of men cheered and muscled to the bar for a glass of cheap beer. Maggie elbowed her way out and took a seat at the table across from Race King. He gave her a smile that she returned.

As she looked at him she saw something in his eyes she hadn't seen before. He cared about her. It wasn't just about getting her to share his bed, but a real honest caring that made her smile.

As the crowd returned to their tables for cards and to enjoy the free beer, Jackson lifted his glass and whistled. "To our Maggie!"

The bar drank the toast, and Maggie stood and lifted her glass of sherry. "To the man who saved my life." Jackson smiled at her but she turned to the aging cowboy at her table. "To Mr. King."

She didn't miss the look of anger that flashed over Jackson's handsome face. She didn't care if she had disappointed him. After all he had disappointed her too.

They settled in to play a hand of poker and Harry Boater gave her a toothy grin and handed her a small leather pouch with a heavy load. "I gathered your winnings this afternoon. So what are you going to do with a practically brand new revival tent, Miss Maggie?"

"Thank you, Harry. I have no idea what to do with a tent."

She had forgotten about the bet and her odd winnings. What was she going to do with a church tent? She could sell it. She had to think about it, but she was going to have to see it first.

"It's still set up outside of town. I'll send a couple of my boys out to watch it tonight. I never trust those Bible thumpers. They're libel to try to sneak it out under cover of darkness." Race said.

"Then I guess I better go and take a look at it tomorrow. Maybe I'll find an elephant and start a circus?"

Later that night, Maggie gathered the money from the bar and the clients headed upstairs with the girls. Cat was taking Harry Boater to the empty room at the end of the hallway, so her room was empty. She headed to the kitchen for a glass of warm milk and found Jackson waiting for her.

"How are you feeling?" he asked.

"I wish people would stop asking me that. I'm tired but I'm fine."

"Want to know how I feel?" he asked and Maggie realized his voice sounded tight and carefully controlled. She instinctively took a couple of steps to put the table between herself and him.

"How do you feel?" she asked softly.

"Embarrassed?"

She heard the sharpness in her tone and so did Jackson. He took a drink from his glass and stared at her.

"Why would you be embarrassed?"

He was angry and she wasn't entirely sure why.

"To see my woman fawning over that old cowboy. It's humiliating."

"I wasn't fawning over anyone. I thanked the man who saved my life. I would think you might be grateful for that too."

"I could have saved you, if I had been standing at your elbow the way that *Poule D'eau* does. He's making a spectacle out of courting you."

"Oh, he isn't courting me, and he isn't that old. He's just kind."

"*C'est des conneries!*" he swore. "How many times has he asked you to take him to your bed?"

She didn't answer that and it only made him angrier. He slammed his glass on the table. "You are my woman, Maggie," he shouted.

"No, I am my woman." She corrected. "I may share

your bed, but I am not your wife or your chattel."

"Then marry me," he said too harshly to be a true proposal. "Become my *femme dévouée*."

She didn't think he was serious, so she wasn't sure how to answer. There was a time when she wanted nothing more than to be his wife, to wake every morning in his arms, to bear his children. But not like this. Not with him scowling at her as if she had been caught stealing from him.

"I have no wish to be anyone's wife, Jackson."

"I know you love me," he said, taking her shoulders in a tight grip.

"And yet a minute ago you accused me of trying to sleep with Race King."

"I'm sorry, but I can't lose you. I love you."

"I love you, and I want to stay with you. Why does anything have to change? Why can't I be here, with you? I can work and keep this place running smoothly for you and we can be happy."

He suddenly pulled her close in a crushing hug. "I can't lose you, *mon cher*."

"Then do not push me, Jackson. I am here because I want to be."

She did return to his bed and found again that glorious heated thrill of his touch, but in her heart she knew it was different, somehow.

March 5th 1880

I wonder if anything will be the same between Jackson and I. The misty veil of novelty has been torn away from our relationship and I fear we will not go back to the way we had been, I share his bed and my body, and I love waking in his arms, but the magic is gone....

The wind ripped at Maggie's expensive French bonnet. The peacock feather danced like a Can-Can girl and Harry Boater snickered behind his hand. She gave him a smile. It was hard not to feel a little silly in all her fine new clothes. But it was nice too. The men gathered to show off her new prize were as interested in her as in the huge tent, its edges flapping in the relentless prairie wind.

"Well, there it is, Miss Maggie. One traveling preacher's circus of God."

It was a wonderful tent, no stains, no tears or sign of wear. It was a clean white with strong wooden ribs and thick ropes. It was the size of the first floor of *La Maison Bleue*, with two towering peaks. It reminded her of the photographs she had seen of the Rocky Mountains. She wandered around the inside, stepping off the size and imagining it with temporary walls. It would work. She could use this tent as a temporary saloon, if she could just get Jackson to see it the way she did.

She had Harry's men take it down and secure it in the large wooden crate used to hold it. They even put in on the back of a wagon and hauled it to the saloon. Jackson met her at the door and she excitedly told him all about it.

He didn't seem nearly as excited but listened as Maggie laid out a plan.

"It's nearly spring, I thought we could go out to Colorado and set up a temporary saloon. A raised wooden floor to set the tent on and throw up a few dividers and we can be making money while a permanent building is going up."

"And who is going to run this new saloon?"

Maggie waited a moment then sighed. "Me! I'll run it for you."

His brow knitted together and his face grew dark. "No."

He turned and walked into the saloon. Maggie followed him to the bar, stunned by the casual way he dismissed the entire idea.

"Why," she asked. "You said yourself that I have done an excellent job."

"You have."

"And Billy is doing so much better that he is coming back in the summer."

"He is." Jackson passed through the bar and into the kitchen. Maggie could hear some of the men in the saloon laughing.

"So what am I supposed to do? Go back to serving beer?"

"You could concentrate on making your man happy," he said, and pulled her close, burying his face in her hair as he pressed kisses to her neck.

"Making you a rich man would make you very happy."

"I'm rich enough, *cher*." He spread a line of hot kisses down her neck and over the exposed upper curve of her breast. His hand cupped her breast. His mouth worked lower pushing down the layers of rich velvet cloth until he found the puckered nipple.

Maggie breath caught in her throat. "Someone will see us."

"No one is looking for us."

"I want to talk about the tent."

"I want to taste that sweet pussy."

He began to lower himself drawing her shirt up her thigh.

"Jackson, please." She pushed at her skirt but he ignored her, pressing kisses to the inside of her thigh. "Just think about all the money we can make in Denver. The silver they are taking out of that territory. I really want to try this. I want to be your partner."

"I don't want a partner." He said trying to move closer to her Venus Mound.

Maggie closed her legs, forcing him away from her. He nearly toppled background. "What about what I want?"

He sighed as if running out of patience. "I want you to do less work, not more, and not hundreds of miles away. I thought we might buy a house and you could set it up. We can have a real home."

Maggie was stunned. Was he asking her to marry him again? He hadn't said the words but a house, a home? She wanted to believe that this was possible. She loved him. She knew the second saloon was a good idea but sharing a life with Jackson was what she wanted most.

She pulled him up and kissed him hard, taking his tongue into her mouth to artfully twist and tangle with it. He moaned against her lips, his hands finding her breast and he rolled the nipple under his thump. It sent a jolt through her body to pool in the folds of her womanhood. The passion she felt for him drowned out all thought and even the voices coming from the saloon.

She lifted her leg, letting Jackson run his hand along her thigh. His fingers found the damp curls at the apex of her legs. He pushed into her, instinctively finding the pleasure spot. He stroked it and kissed her, catching every gasp and moan until Maggie shook in his arms.

Maggie kissed him, her hands going to the buttons of his pants and just as she found his hardened flesh, Bud's voice came from the corner.

"Boss you need to come out here."

"Go away, Bud."

Maggie pulled his swollen penis from his pants.

"It's important, Jackson. Someone is here," Buddy sounded a little desperate.

"Give them a drink and make them wait."

Maggie began to pull at him, drawing out the pleasure.

"It's Madam Bajoliere."

Jackson jerked away from her and stood stock still for a moment. He tucked himself into his pants and ran a nervous hand over his bald head.

"Your mother is here?" Maggie asked.

"No. Stay here."

He straightened his shirt and pants and hurried out the hallway.

Maggie heard his voice as he greeted her. He was forcibly cheerful and unnecessarily loud. It made him sound even more nervous. She was stunned but after straightening her skirt and bodice she followed him into the barroom.

No one noticed her as she slipped through the doorway, but she noticed the woman standing in front of Jackson. She was young, beautiful, her eyes flashing fire at Jackson. An older Negro woman stood quietly beside her.

Madam couldn't be his mother.

55

It hit Maggie like a rock to her skull.

She wasn't his mother. She was his wife.

Maggie was the other woman, his concubine, his whore.

She suddenly felt sick to her stomach.

"Where is this M. McGregor?" the woman shouted.

Maggie silently wished the floor would open up and swallow her. All eyes in the saloon turned to Maggie and a sudden hush came over the place. Why did she want to hide? She had not broken any vows, told any lies, broken any hearts. She took a step forward and took a deep breath.

"I'm Maggie."

Madam Bajoliere took a step forward to meet her and raised her hand to slap her and the room seemed to erupt. Maggie realized what she was doing and grabbed her hand.

"Madam," she said. "I understand your anger. I don't blame you, but you are not the only person who was deceived here."

The woman looked at her and blinked her rather large eyes. Maggie had a chance to really look at her and she was surprised by what she saw. She was young, probably a year or two older than Maggie, and very pretty. Her honey colored hair was perfectly coiffed but her dark eyes snapped.

"Are you saying that you were lied to as well?" she asked.

"Of course, I am a lot of things but I have no desire to steal a man from his lawful wife."

Jackson finally seemed jolted out of his shock and he came forward and stepped between the combatants.

"Too little, too late, Jackson," Maggie said, turning

toward the door. She could hear Jackson's wife shouting in Cajun French, he was shouting back, but Maggie didn't wait to listen.

Her heart was aching. Her head thumped like a steam engine and she wanted to scream.

How stupid could she be? How could she think that what she had with Jackson was real? How could she trust him so easily?

She walked the length of the boardwalk and stopped beside the wagon loaded down with the tent she'd won in the poker game. She leaned against the wagon's edge and let the tears flow. She had trusted him, loved him, given herself to him body and soul.

She gripped the edge of the wagon and her body began to shake. She had been a fool and she would never be a fool again.

Catherine stopped beside her and put an arm around her shoulder. "Are you all right?"

"No," she said. "I feel ridiculous."

Cat gave her a hug. "I know how you feel. We both had our hearts torn up."

"We were both lied to." Maggie said hugging her hard.

"What do we do about this?" Cat asked wiping away Maggie's tears and then her own.

Maggie took a deep breath and squared her shoulders. "I have nearly three hundred dollars saved and I have a tent. I am going west. I can open my own saloon. I'll make my fortune."

"I'll go with you."

This time there were no tears when they hugged.

The saloon was quiet when Maggie and Cat returned. The men at the bar looked sheepish. Maggie was certain the entire story of her relationship with Jackson had been laid out in front of everyone. Buddy behind the bar gave her a weak smile.

"Can I get you something, sugar?"

"I could use a glass of the good stuff."

He poured her the glass of the rich amber colored bourbon and she sipped the harsh liquid. It burned a trail down her throat but somehow it only strengthened her resolve.

"How can I get to Colorado?" she asked no one in particular.

"The trails are well marked and with spring coming, there are plenty of others headed that direction," someone said.

"You ain't leaving us, are you, Maggie?" another asked.

"I'm afraid I've worn out my welcome."

There was a general rumbling of dissatisfaction among the men, some of whom probably hoped that Maggie would be taking on customers now that things had gone so wrong with Jackson. But one thing was certain, no matter what she did in the future, she was never going to make Jackson a single dollar on her back.

From the end of the bar, Race King watched her. She found she couldn't look at him. He had been so kind to her, even when he ask her to come to his bed; he had been a gentleman about it.

But he only smiled and lifted a glass to salute her. "You'll be dearly missed," he said softly.

She was done here and it only made sense to move ahead. But first she had to talk to Jackson.

March 6th 1880

I feel like such a fool. But this feeling is the fire I need to push me out this door and into my own life. I cannot stay here another moment, but I have to face Jackson one last time....

Maggie sat on the edge of her bed, most of her things had been packed and she had purchased a wagon large enough to ship her crated tent... but how would she get herself and Cat as far as Denver? And how would she find the best place to set up her tent and pursue her new life?

After telling the men in the saloon she was leaving, she knew it was just a matter of time before he knocked on her bedroom door. Cat had taken Harry Boater to the room at the end of the hall.

So she was alone in her room, dressed in the most elegant silk dressing gown and robe that the local dressmaker had in her shop. She had bought it for Jackson but now she wore it for herself. To reminder her that she was worth the finest things life had to offer, even if she had to get them for herself.

At just a little after nine p.m. a light tapping on the door made her jump. The door opened and Jackson's handsome face appeared.

"Is your wife settled in?" Maggie asked.

"I'm sorry," he said simply. The strange thing was she believed him. He was sorry. He did care about her and she hadn't asked the right questions before she fell into his bed. That mistake was on her.

"I know. I ask you a lot of questions, how to pleasure a man, I just never thought to ask if the man I was pleasuring was married. Why did you ask me to marry you?"

"I love you," he said, rushing toward her. But Maggie stopped him.

"I love you too, Jackson. Would you have married me knowing you had a legal wife back in Louisiana?"

"I don't know. But I love you and when Marie goes back to New Orleans, I'll buy you a fine house here in town and we can go back to the way we were."

Maggie laughed but moved away. "I have no desire to play second fiddle to your Madam."

"Then what do you want?" He was losing his patience—as much as he wanted to convince her to stay, in his life, in his house, in his bed.

"It not about what I want, Jackson. That is never going to happen now. What I am going to do is move it Colorado and set up my tent."

"Your tent?"

"Yes. It's my tent. And you wouldn't dare try to claim it."

"I want you to stay." His voice was a plaintive whine. "*Je t'aime.*"

She thought about it for a moment. "No, I want possibilities. I want to make choices based on truth. You never gave me the truth."

"I wanted to tell you everything. I wanted to be honest. I married Marie when we were young. She was one of my mother's girls and I thought I loved her. I can't get a divorce. We're Catholic."

"You can marry a whore but you can't divorce one. You can make a woman a whore but you can't marry her."

"I didn't make you a whore!" he shouted.

"No, I did." She turned and put the last of her things into an open trunk at the foot of her bed. "And now I am going to make myself a rich whore."

"You'll leave here with only the things you brought with you," he snarled grabbing her hand to stop her.

"Jackson," she said softly. "I have done your books for months. I can take anything I want. Now take your hand off me."

He dropped her hand and sat heavily on the side of the bed. "What shall I do without you, *mon cheri?*"

"I suspect you will get along just fine." She cupped a hand to his face and felt him lean into her touch. "You will find some other young, innocent girl and teach her how to love you, the way you did me."

"It will never be the same," he said sadly.

"Good."

"When will you leave?"

"Tomorrow."

"Will you spend the night with me, mon amour?"

"No. You should go to the hotel and sleep with your wife." She watched him walk out the door and close it behind him.

A part of her heart that she hoped would soon die hurt more than she could stand. She sat at the dressing table and cried until there were no tears left.

Jackson left the saloon by the back stairs. Maggie supposed he would do his best to mend things with his wife. She waited until she was certain he was not going to come back, and then went to the kitchen for something to eat. She stirred the coals and filled the firebox of the stove and set the coffee pot on to boil.

She found some bread and a jar of jelly. She carved some of the cold roast beef. She put it all on a tray and turned to find the negro woman that had come to the saloon with Madam Bajoliere standing there. She looked tired and harried. There was a purple bruise on her cheek and her lip was cut.

"Are you all right?"

"Yes'em. Just a mite sore's all."

"Good heavens. Are you bleeding?" Maggie gasped.

She touched a finger to her lip and winced. "No. The bleedin' stopped early this morning."

Maggie poured a cup of hot coffee and sat it in front of her. "Who did this to you?"

"Madam. She was powerful angry at you and the Mister." She looked at the coffee and Maggie slid it closer, so there was no doubt it was hers.

"What did that have to do with you?"

"Nothing. I was just in the way when the fury had nowhere else to go."

Maggie pulled a face. "I guess I should have let her slap me."

For a moment the two looked at each other and then the older woman started to laugh.

"You're a pip, Miss Maggie. You are."

"What's your name?"

"Bella Gillard."

Maggie slid the tray, the one she intended for her guest upstairs, toward the woman. "Are you hungry?"

She said nothing but started to pick at the roast beef.

"How long a have you worked for Madam?"

"I went to her when she married the mister seven

years ago, before that I worked for her Mam and before that I was owned by her Mam. And there weren't no before that."

"Are you happy with her?" Maggie asked.

Miss Gilliard raised a brow. "Do I look happy?"

The shared another laugh.

"Would you like to work for me?" Maggie asked, taking a piece of the roast beef. "I need a personal maid and someone to help me set up my saloon in Colorado."

"You'll pay me?

"Certainly. A fair wage."

The woman ate the roast beef and smiled. "I think I'd like working for you, Miss Maggie."

Maggie sent Bella to gather her things and told her to come back and stay at the saloon for the night. There was no reason for Jackson's furious wife to vent her spleen on the woman for wanting out. It took a lot to take a beating, make a decision, and make a change. If she could do it then, by God, so could Maggie.

So she took out the new dress, the red satin and tulle with the deeply plunging neckline and the pleats gathered in the skirt that showed off half her stockinged leg. She dressed her hair and powdered her nose then slipped into a pair of red velvet slippers.

The men gathered around the bar stopped when she stepped onto the top step. Her dress made a soft swishing sound as it swirled around her ankles. The smell of sweet cigar smoke wafted over her, more potent than any French perfume. The noises hushed as she took each step slowly, deliberately. Every eye followed her as she descended the stairs.

She understood the power of sex, had seen it in her own life. But now she could feel it, the power coursing through her. It was more than sex, or power, or control.

It was strength, and it was all hers.

The hush was replaced by a rumble of voices as she walked to the bar, the yards of red velvet swaying with the rhythm of her hips. At the bar Buddy gave her a glass of bourbon, it was watered down but still the good stuff. The men had gathered around but no one was talking.

She sipped the drink and smiled. "It's too quiet in here. Opal, why don't you play something we can dance to?"

Opal took a seat at the piano and began a polka. All the girls were partnered up and Harry Boater led Maggie to the open floor. Buddy took a turn with her in the Virginia Reel. Finally, it was Race that took her hand for a waltz.

Jackson didn't come into the saloon that night and Maggie reveled in being the hostess. She made sure all drinks were filled and everyone was laughing and happy. And if she didn't feel happy herself, she didn't let it show until Race took a seat across from her and reached for her hand.

"You look lovely, girl."

"Thank you. I feel lovely."

She motioned for the cards and set up Cat with a table of eager players, then returned to her chair across from Race King.

"You have them eating out of your hand," he said with a smile.

"I don't want them eating. I want them drinking, and laughing and dancing and spending money."

"You are a smart girl."

"I have to be smart, being stupid only gives you pain."

As the evening came to a close, the girls went upstairs with their partners. Maggie sorted out the money and shooed the last stragglers out the doors. Race started to rise and she motioned for him to wait and she locked the doors.

"Well, you got it all planned out, but do you think you can take yourself, maybe a couple of women and a wagon full of tent to Colorado?" he asked.

"I'll try. How do I do that?"

He raised a brow. "I could take you."

"Could you?"

"I am taking a herd of cattle to Fort Collins, you can get a covered wagon and we'll get you and your load to Denver, but if you really want to make money you might want to go to one of the silver mining towns."

She leaned over the table and kissed him on the mouth.

The cowboy watched her as she turned and walked to the stairs. She stopped and held out her hand to him. "Would you like to join me, Mr. King?"

A smile broke over his face. He took off his dusty hat and left it on the table as he followed her up the steps.

Part Two

Where the Heart Lives

August 8th 1880

We have settled in Boulder, Colorado. A more beautiful place in the world cannot exist. We have set up the tent and are bringing in a healthy amount of money while the timber frame of my beautiful building is going up. There are few permanent residences to this small town, but the silver mines have begun to produce huge amounts, and the men will come....

It seemed to her that the sun shone brighter on Maggie's face here than it had back in New Philadelphia, Ohio or even in Ogallala, Nebraska. She stood outside the tent, the sleeves of her chambray shirt were rolled up her arms and dust covered her cowboy boots and the hem of her heavy work skirt. She beat at the dust with her Stetson hat but it did little to remove the dirt.

The lanky cowboy of nearly fifty years stood beside her looking at the workers as they climbed the three story frame.

"You happy with all this?" he asked.

"Beyond happy, Race. Beyond happy." She used the hat to block the sun so she could look up at him. "And you, Mr. King, are you happy?"

"I'm certainly impressed, girly."

He had started to call her that shortly after their first night together. He had come to her rescue, in a way, after the humiliation of having her relationship with Jackson Bajoliere made public. He had offered her a one way trip out of Ogallala, Nebraska and offered to help her set up her temporary tent. Then, he had shocked her by going back to Nebraska to sell everything, from his ranch to his stock.

He had explained that he had no family and was a rich enough man to start over anywhere. He bought a tract of land, intending to build a new ranch and purchased five hundred head of stock. The new King Ranch was located just ten miles out of town and a day's ride from Fort Collins. He was poised to become even richer. He had built a small cabin on the site and was moving on to barns and stockyards.

Maggie was just grateful for his strong shoulder to lean on and his wise advice to make her dream of the new saloon, the Silver Filly, come true.

It surprised everyone how many of the girls had decided to forgo the security of Jackson's established business. Catherine, Opel and Callie had come with Maggie, and along the way they picked up a pretty young blonde calling herself Sally Bingham. A couple more girls would be recruited once the building was done.

At night the big tent came alive.

The music played, the whiskey flowed and the money rolled in.

After the crowds were gone and the girls were off to the separate little wooden stalls they had built in the back of the tent, Maggie would ride to the cabin with Race.

One clear night, the stars twinkled overhead and the soft mountain air blew up the valley and ruffled the tuffs of hair that came untucked from her cowboy hat. After a while she took off the hat and tossed it into the back of the wagon with the days supplies.

She turned to Race and slid a hand into his shirt front.

"Well, girly, aren't you getting frisky?"

"Yes, I am, sir."

She ran a hand over his chest and brushed her fingers over his nipple. "You need to either speed that pony to a gallop or slow him to a walk?"

"Why's that?" he asked, leaning close to give her a kiss on the lips. She took off his hat and threw it into the wagon with hers.

"Cause I'm about to do something dangerous."

She took off her boots and reached under her skirt to slide off her bloomers.

He gave a slow whistle and slowed the horse to a walk. "This is the sort of thing that gets old men hurt."

"Old men never do things like this, Race." She reached over and unbuttoned the fly of his jeans. He was already starting to get hard as she reached in and freed his member. Maggie unbuttoned her blouse and untied her chemise. She stood and let him move his hands and the reins to either side of him. She sat on his lap and began to play with his penis.

"You're going to make me drive this wagon into a ditch."

"I'm going to make you come like a shotgun."

She rubbed his member until he was swollen and beads of jism formed on his tip. She slid up and took his hard dick into her soft flesh. She pumped her hips back and forth, kissing his hard jaw and his soft lips, nuzzling his neck. Her bare breasts pressed against him, drawing his attention from the road. He kissed the peak of one nipple as it sway seductively in front of him.

Maggie unpinned her hair and Race groaned. Before long, he dropped the reins and wrapping his arms around her, pulled her back on to the sacks of feed grain in the back of the wagon. He knelt between her legs and pushed deep into her over and over, until she was gasping and panting and finally they climaxed together.

They peeked up over the edge of the wagon and found the horse had wandered into an open field and was contentedly munching away in a field of red clover and buffalo grass.

Maggie looked at Race and started to laugh. After a few minutes he joined in.

"At least we're not in a ditch," he said, doing up his pants.

"I never doubted old Ginger's common sense. She knows better than to distract us from our fun."

"Fun!" he said with a laugh. "Every time I touch you, I'm serious. Marry me, Maggie."

"No. I love you too much to marry you."

Sept 30th 1880

The house is going up fast and soon Race and I will have a home for our business. I cannot wait to hand him the first of the profits. I want him to see that all his faith in me is justified....

The following morning, Maggie took the wagon and headed back to town to oversee the rising of the second floor walls. It was getting easier to visualize the way it would look in the end. A majestic three story with multi-paned glass windows and gingerbread trim, it would rise over all the other buildings in town. She had already ordered gallons of white and pale blue paint and a full size statue of a rearing filly, completely clad in silver plate that would stand at one end of the twenty five foot bar. The first floor would have a kitchen, storage, and dining room in the back, and the entire front of the house would a huge bar with a small raised stage at one end and the massive bar at the other.

The second floor would have a gallery behind a turned wood railing. It was open to the bar below and lined with six comfortable bedrooms, one for each of her hard working girls. There would be two larger ones at either end. One would be a bath house, with four copper tubs and a hot water heating coal stove and one was a bunk house with stacked beds that could be rented by the night or the week.

But the third floor would be tucked beneath the wide gabled roof and would hold a private apartment for Maggie, with a bedroom, sitting room and office, and a private bathroom. Bella had her own suit of rooms off the apartment. The apartment would be accessible by a private staircase directly to the first floor back porch and a set of steps it would share with one additional large third floor bedroom that Maggie intended for Catherine, which led to the second floor landing.

It was a breathtaking vision, and Race and Maggie were determined to see it realized.

The men of the small town of Boulder watched in awe as the Silver Filly slowly rose from the valley floor. Before long, outsiders from as far away as Denver and Leadsville were sending telegraphs inquiring when the place would open. And powerbrokers from as far as Chicago were making plans to travel to the new attraction.

Maggie answered each request with a promise that by the time the weather turned cold the Silver Filly would be heating up.

The second floor walls went up fast and the foreman of the construction crew stopped his men to eat lunch. Leon Gable was handsome and strong, a talented carpenter and he loved to flirt with his beautiful young employer.

"Afternoon, boss lady."

"Good afternoon, Mr. Gable. She's looking better and better."

"Yes, she is, and her owner is looking good too."

Leon was a big strapping fellow, not more than thirty years old, with a head of chestnut hair and big blue eyes. He was the sort of man that made the girls who worked for Maggie swoon.

Callie had been batting her eyes at the big carpenter for days, but only Cat had managed to get him into her bed. And he had sung her praises for days. Now, it seemed that her foreman was turning his attention to Maggie. She hated to discourage anyone who wanted to give her money, but these days, she was only sleeping with Race, and had no intention of taking on anyone new.

He moved closer and asked her if there was anything he could do to make her happier. Maggie smiled up at him.

"Build faster."

"You're a slave driver, woman. Maybe you need a distraction. Get your mind off the work and on a little pleasure."

"You forget, Leon. My work is pleasure." She walked to the wagon and took out the blueprints again.

"How soon will the third floor be up?"

"At this rate? Later today." He said following her. "The masons are coming in day after tomorrow and first of the two chimneys will start to go up on Friday."

"Make sure you bring them up to the tent that night. I'll make sure they get a proper welcome."

"And what do I get?"

"Well, I think any of my girls would be more than happy to make you more than happy."

Race rode into the yard on his beautiful quarter horse, he called Old Jasper. It had been fathered by the famous Whalebone and cost him a small fortune, but he was a great stock animal.

"Hello, Boss," Leon said, moving a respectable distance from Maggie.

"Leon was just telling me the mason will start on the two main chimneys this Friday," she said, smiling up at Race.

"And the kitchen stove will be ready to go next week," the carpenter threw in.

Race nodded agreement as he reached out a hand to help Maggie up onto the rump of the big horse. "Sounds good. Thought I'd take you back to the tent for some lunch."

Maggie pressed a kiss to his cheek and settled in with him between her legs. "See you later, Leon."

As they rode away Race dropped a hand to her leg and gave it a squeeze. "Are you happy with the work on the house?"

"Yes. I think it's going up fast. But then I've never built a house before."

As they rode across town to the tent, Maggie teased Race by sliding her hand toward his crotch.

"Now girl, you're gonna end up in a field again."

"Promise?" she purred in his ear.

But he looked serious as he helped her off the horse and into the tent.

"What do you think about Leon Gable?" he asked her as she took a seat in the tent.

Bella brought them each a plate of cold fried chicken and roasted carrots from the kitchen garden.

"He seems to be a good carpenter."

"That ain't what I mean."

Bella pulled a face. "He's a sweet talking bullshit artist."

Maggie rolled her eyes. "He's a man."

Bella walked back to the kitchen and Maggie covered Race's big work-worn hand with hers. "Why are you asking about Leon?"

Race took a bit of chicken and chewed silently, then wiped his mouth with one of the white cotton napkins. "He's the sort of man that ought to be sharing a bed with a pretty young thing like you. Not some worn out old cowhand like me."

Maggie stared at him. Every now and then he would say things like that, about his age, and how she should be with some other man.

"You're more than enough man for me, Race King. I don't want any younger man. I sure don't need any younger man. You think a younger man can make me quiver more than you. A younger man can make me pant harder, or come faster? You make me ache, Race, and you are all I want."

She leaned over the table and planted a kiss on his mouth, then opened her mouth, slipping her tongue over his lip, deepening the kiss until she was breathless. "I love you, Race King," she whispered in his ear and he gave her a smile. "And I only want you."

He picked up her hand a kissed it.

That night, Maggie slid into bed next to Race and smiled as he wrapped his strong arms around her. She loved feeling safe and secure, just lying next to him. He always made her feel like she was the only woman in the world who mattered. But she wasn't sure what she gave him in return.

Sex?

A warm body?

It seemed a very unfair trade. She got so much and all he got was her. She rolled to face him and he kissed her softly on the mouth.

"You didn't mean what you said, did you?" she asked softly.

"When? Earlier?"

"You don't want me to sleep with Leon Gable do you?"

"No, girly. If it was up to me you'd never have to sleep with another man you didn't care about."

She sat up and turned to face him. "Well, I don't sleep with anyone now that I don't want to. I only want you Race."

She lifted her satin gown over her head and sat naked next to him on the bed. She rolled him to his back and ran her hands down his chest trailing her nails through the matted fur scattered over his chest. As he lay back on the bed, Maggie kissed his neck and lower, taking her time so that the tension built. He closed his eyes as she took his growing erection in her hands and then into her mouth.

He groaned as she drew him in and out, sucking him deeper each time. He was not like Jackson, hard as a rock and ready to go at a moment's notice. It took a little time, some play and gentle teasing to get him hard as granite. She loved giving him that, loved taking him into her mouth and hearing him moan in anticipation of what came next. She worked him harder and harder until he was pulling at her, dragging her back up his long lean body.

She crawled up, straddling his hips and rubbing her moist core against the underside of his erection.

"My God, girl, you're so beautiful."

"And so are you, all tight muscles and man fur."

He smiled and she rocked her hips, rubbing her trimmed muff against his hard cock. He growled her name and Maggie laughed. This time when she rocked forward she pulled the tip of his dick downward and slid it into her moist core.

"Oh God, darin'."

She took him deep inside her and rocked back, shifting him inside her. A few more quick strokes and sweat broke out on his upper lip. He leaned forward and ran his lips over her tender breast. The peaks puckered and begged his attention. He gave it, cupping them and lifting them to his mouth. He kissed them and drew the pebbled nipples into his mouth, as Maggie leaned back to let him taste her.

"I love you, Race," she said as his hard member dragged over her throbbing flesh.

"I love you too, Maggie," he grunted, then lifted himself into her again and again.

She rocked harder faster, taking him deep and dragging him over her engorged flower over and over, until he gritted his teeth and bucked hard. Maggie felt his hot release flood her and bore down hard until her climax exploded. She arched her back, threw her head back and screamed his name.

She collapsed on him, hugging him close to her naked body.

Race gathered her close and stroked her arm with his work-roughened hand.

"I never want you to leave me, girl."

Maggie yawned sleepily and cuddled closer. 'I never will."

"Marry me, Maggie."

"I love you too much to marry you."

November 3rd 1880

I am starting to see the house in the construction rubble. I believe there is no more perfect place in the world than Boulder, Colorado. The view from the front of the building is breathtaking. I am thrilled to be so breathless....

Race stood on the newly laid oak floor of the first floor and stared up at the timber frame still visible above. The walls were nearly done, the roof was on and the decisions about details needed to be made. As usual Maggie had him there to help her decide. Mr. Corbey was the fellow who was responsible for coating the walls with plaster. He wanted to do most of the interior rooms but Maggie wasn't sure she wanted to lose the timber.

"What does closing in the frame actually do for the house?" Maggie asked. She like the big timber frame and hated the thought of covering it with the pine boards, even with a beautiful coat of paint.

"Well, it will hold the heat in better on those cold winter days and nights. We can even pack it with cotton to do a better job."

"It might be worth the extra work, girly." Race suggested.

"Your pa's right about that, Miss," the man said. "It will make the whole house warmer in the winter and cooler in the heat of summer."

Maggie looked at Race and laughed. A smile broke over his craggy face and he looked away.

"My pa? How could you think this incredibly handsome gentleman is my father?" She planted a kiss on Race's mouth. His smile widened.

Mr. Corbey's face slowly began to turn a deep red, he fumbled for something to say. "I meant no offense… I just assumed…

Race took pity on the man. "No offense taken, my friend. I was not lucky enough to have children of my own, but the All Mighty saw fit to send me this angel into my life anyway."

Now it was Maggie's turn to blush. She wasn't a wife, and she didn't want to be, even an accidental one, but the idea that she made him so happy was a joy to her. Maggie wound her arm around his and pulled him close. "I was the lucky one, my darling."

Mr. Corbey smiled and the fire in his cheeks began to fade. "Well, then Mrs. King, the final say is yours."

Race gave Maggie a squeeze. "If she loves the hard wood, we find a way to keep the hardwood."

The plastering was decided and the work continued. Maggie watched as the massive bar was set up on the beautiful oak floor. And the brass boot rail, imported from New York City was installed. Maggie lifted the hem of her dress and set her cowboy boot on it and the gathered workmen cheered.

It took weeks to complete but the Silver Filly celebrated its grand opening in late October, just as the snow was beginning to fly in the high mountain town. The men lined up at the bar, Maggie had all the girls outfitted in dresses that would have made the highest Duchess in Jolly Ole' England pea green with envy. She had chosen an elegant purple dress that hugged her toned body, flaring out at her knees and brushing the floor, with a deeply scooped neck and an ostrich feather dyed to match. A length of purple tulle swooped around her shoulders, drawing more attention to the pale mounds of her nearly exposed breasts than they hid.

"You look like a queen," Bella said as Maggie dabbed a touch of French perfume on her wrists.

"The Queen of Nerves maybe?"

"The saloon's full of high mucky-mucks, lawyers, land brokers, the governor's down there drinking bourbon, and smokin' the biggest cigars I've ever seen."

Maggie slipped a gold bracelet on her wrist and smiled. "We need to work on your diction."

"My dick-what?"

Maggie laughed. "Never mind. Are you coming down to have some champagne with me?"

She ran a hand down the front of her black bombazine dress. "Me? Naw. I ain't got no place rubbing elbows with them mucky-mucks."

"Those mucky-mucks." Never mind. Go look on your bed, put it on and meet me down stairs in twenty minutes."

The housekeeper stared at her.

"Go!" Maggie said, shooing her into her own apartment. Then, squaring her shoulders she started down the stairs.

December 5th 1880

How did I get here? Less than three years ago I was a starving teacher and now I am ready to face a room full of dandies all waiting for me to appear. And all I can think about is how badly I want to impress Race. How much I want him to be proud of me. How important he is to everything I do….

Her foot hit the top step and a hush fell over the bar. The band she had brought in from Denver began to play and the crowd picked up the tune, singing "for she's a jolly good fellow" as she descended the stairs. Cat gave her a fluted glass of bubbling champagne.

"To the amazing woman that brought us this incredible place, Maggie McGregor," Cat said.

"Maggie!" they shouted.

She smiled and her gaze searched the crowd for the one face she needed to see. And he was nowhere to be found.

She did her best to meet everyone. She arranged some clandestine meetings for Governor Dawes and Cat. She assured lawyers that she would tell no one the details of their peccadilloes. She toasted the winners at poker and after hours of celebrating, wrapped herself in a warm cloak and called the stable boy, Benny, to bring her a carriage around.

"Where we going, Miss Maggie?" the young man

asked.

"Take me to the King Ranch."

She had nearly fallen asleep when the coach came to a stop and Benny helped her down. The house was dark but she knew the door was not barred. She stepped into the warmth and found Race sitting by the fireplace in a plaid robe and leather slippers she had gotten him for his birthday.

"You look beautiful, girly," he said.

"Don't you girly me," she snapped. "Where were you?"

"I was right here," he said taking a sip of his nightly whiskey.

"You missed our big night," she said, throwing off the cloak.

He rose from the rocker and smiled. "Well, look at you. You are the most beautiful woman I have ever seen."

Tears gathered in her eyes. "Why didn't you come? I wanted you beside me."

"That's not exactly my crowd. Oh honey, why the tears."

"They aren't my crowd either, Race." She wanted to stomp her foot. "I wanted you to see how successful I can be. I'm not just a worthless whore."

He crossed the room and took her by the shoulders. "Hey, now. I never thought of you as worthless. And I most certainly never thought of you as a whore. You're my girl. I love you. And my god, girl. Look at you."

"I missed you tonight. It wasn't much fun without you."

"That's a pretty lie."

"How about you help me out of this monstrosity,"

she said turning her back to him.

His calloused fingers slowly worked the row of fine ivory buttons down her back. As the velvet fabric peeled away, his fingers lingered on the velvety softness of her skin. His hands were warm and worked a sort of magic on her frazzled nerves. She didn't realize how much tension she felt until it began to drain away. He kneaded the tight muscles of her shoulders.

"Was it wonderful?" he asked, and pressed a gentle kiss to her neck.

"It was crowded and loud and we will make a lot of money."

He slid the dress off her shoulders and trailed kisses over the exposed skin. He worked his hand up her neck and into the soft tendrils of hair that escaped her up do. He let the dress fall off her body and it slithered to the floor with a soft hiss.

Race pulled the bow from the laces of the corset Bella had fought her into and began to untie the ribbon. Maggie gave a contented sigh as she was freed from the whale bone contraception.

She stood in the light of the flickering fire, naked and warmed by his heated gaze. He stepped back and watched her bend over, the curve of her buttocks turned at just the perfect angle for him to admire. She toed off her satin slippers and slowly began to roll her silk stocking down.

Race made a soft whistle, and she grinned as his growing erection moved the flaps of his robe.

She rolled the second stocking down, bending slowly to give him that perfect view again.

Race pulled her back against him and pulled the handful of pins from her hair and it fell down her back swirling like smoke around her waist.

Maggie pulled the belt of the robe and pushed it off his broad shoulders.

Race slide an arm under her knees and lifted her, carrying her across the room to the big bed. The small cabin was little more than a sitting room with a bed, but in his arms it felt like a suite at the Palmer House in Chicago.

He laid her down and Maggie reached out and slid her hand between his legs, cupping his manhood. He groaned as she curled her fingers around his scrotum.

She slid down his naked body and drew him to her mouth. He told her once that he had never had a woman love him as she had, had never done the things she had done and no woman had ever made him as hard she did. She liked the idea of that. She took him into her mouth and then out and each time she took him deeper. He pulled her away and kissed her mouth deeply.

Maggie was concentrating on bringing him pleasure, wanting to make him happy. Race surprised her by turning her so that he could return her gift. His strong hands parted her legs and he lowered his mouth to her womanhood. He ran his tongue along her damp folds and into the lips of her labia. Maggie bucked in shock but the feeling flooded her system so fast that her reaction was so take him deeper. She groaned against his hard shaft.

They were lying face to face, their mouths probing each other's sensitive genitals.

Her body grew hot and sweat began to speckle her skin, making her hands slick. She reached around his hips, grabbing Race's buttocks and pulled him closer, until the entire shaft of his penis was in her mouth and deep into her throat. She took him all and dropped her knees to the mattress, giving him more access. He did the same, cupping her backside and drove his tongue into her flesh. He licked her swollen clitoris, nibbling and flicking it with his teeth and tongue.

Maggie rocked her hips and, holding him tight as they both exploded in powerful climax.

He rolled away from her, his hand finding hers in the tangle of sheets.

"Dear God, girly. That was incredible."

"I'm still throbbing," she said weakly. "I feel wonderful."

He spun her to meet him and they curled up naked as they day they were born.

Race kissed her ear. "Just think all those men tonight wanted to be the one you choose to give your beautiful self to. And you chose a broken down old cowboy."

"I chose a man so powerful he makes my body scream. I love you, Race."

Slowly, they dropped off to sleep.

Sometime in the night, Race slipped out and padded naked to the stone fireplace. He built a crackly fire and slipped back in against her warm skin. Maggie rolled into his arms and watched the firelight dance over the planes of his face. The corners of his finely molded mouth turned up slightly and after a while his pale blue eyes closed. He looked content and it made Maggie heart swell. She had believed herself in love with Jackson, but this feeling in her heart was unmistakable. He was her everything, She wanted him, needed him, loved him and she would move heaven and earth for him. He was such a good man.

Doubt ran through her soul like a frightened rabbit. It skipped through the part of herself that she hated, her fear that she was somehow damaged and would never be good enough for a man like this. Why was he curled in the bed of a small cabin with a saloon whore?

"Race," she said, and pulled closer to him. Needing the reassuring warmth of his strong body. "Why don't you have a family?"

"I got a family," he said. "Had a mother and father, a handful of brothers and even a kid sister, back in Indiana."

"I mean a wife and children?"

The contented smile on his face faded. He took a deep breath that Maggie thought she could feel all the way to her toes. Maggie rested her head on his chest and heard the steady beat of his heart.

"I had a wife, once, years ago." He sounded sad. "Her name was May. She was pretty as a button, smart and a little sassy. We were married for almost two years. She caught a lung fever and died. We never had any children."

Suddenly she was sorry she had asked. She had no business prying into his life. No right to disturb his memories.

"I'm sorry."

"It was a sorry time." He wrapped his arms around her and pulled her as close as she could get.

"Tell me about her," Maggie asked and buried her nose in the warm curve of his neck.

"Not much to tell. She was pretty, not a beauty like you but she had a sweet face too. She could sing like an angel but she had a temper. She worked like a man, slept like a stone and snored like a stream engine."

Maggie giggled at that.

"She got sick in late December. We were miles from any of our kin. When the weather broke I loaded her up in a wagon and took her to town, nearly a day's ride. She died a week later, and her family blamed me. Maybe rightly?"

"Sounds like you did everything you could. Sometimes bad things happen. It's no one's fault. Do you miss her?"

He looked thoughtful for moment. "I did, for a long time. Missed not having sons and not having heirs for all I built up. But then I wandered into a saloon and saw this beautiful girl dealing poker and selling the worst whiskey I ever drank."

"A whore's not much of a substitute for a family," she said softly.

He turned to his side and took her arms in his hands. "Now listen to me, girly. You need to stop calling yourself that. I ask you to marry me a dozen times in the last year. I'm more than happy to make you my wife. You keep turning me down. So, no more of that. I don't want to hear it again."

She looked sheepish and when he let her go she curled in against his side.

"Promise me, I won't hear it again," he said.

"I promise," she said against the soft fur of his chest.

He kissed her mouth and hugged her tight. "Now, tell me about your big night, were there a lot of swells there, spending money?"

"Just a few. But there was a governor."

He looked at her and smiled. "A governor? Well,

nice to see that our state is heading is a good direction."

"As long as they pass through our business they can head any direction they want."

Maggie began to touch him gently under the covers, stoking the length of him. She cooed in his ear, making him hard. As she did she felt herself grow wet. He was tender and thorough and if his body wasn't as hard or as perfectly toned as Jackson she knew that she meant something to him. Race was dear to her heart, and good to her body. His touch skimmed over her body, drawing her into a web of desire. He lowered his mouth to her breast. He had a way of drawing his tongue slowly over her nipple that made her breath catch in her throat. He sucked her into his mouth and drew hard on the swollen nipple and Maggie groaned.

Race rose to his knees, parting Maggie's legs, and slowly slid into her welcoming body. He drew her up, supporting her back as Maggie wrapped her arms around his broad shoulders. She clung to him as he drew himself in and out of her, slowly at first then faster and faster.

He whispered her name in her ear. Telling her over and over how dear she was, how he loved her, how much he wanted her, how he ached for her.

Maggie heard his devotion, felt his connection deeper than sex and she melted at the words. She tightened herself around his shaft and held him close. He took her to the mattress and laid her out on the soft cotton sheets. Maggie cocked her hips forward and let him drive into her over and over, pushing her closer and closer to a climax that shook her body and made her scream out his name. Race orgasmed and collapsed onto the bed next to her.

January 25th 1881

The winter passed in a blur of parties, poker, music and merriment. The house made money, the girls made money and everyone was happy. I spent my days working with the girls and my nights sleeping in the arms of the man I had come to love more dearly than anything. I look forward to the New Year like a child, hoping for all my dreams to come true....

Race sat at his usual table in the bar watching as Maggie moved around the room. He kept a close eye on everything that took place, even going so far as to escort a drunken cowboy out the door or put a disgruntled gambler in his place. Maggie came to count on his steady reliable presence.

For his part, Race asked her to marry him once a week. But she always told him he could do better, that he could have a proper bride who he could show off in public. One night while curled in each other's arms he offered to take her to Paris, France. Maggie laughed.

"What would we do in France that we can't do here?" she asked.

"You could see the sights and shop."

She thought for a moment and started to giggle. "I can't picture you shopping in Paris."

"I can picture you trying on the latest fashions. I can picture taking you back to an expensive hotel where you take them all off for me."

They talked about traveling and Maggie found something, beside the farm and the saloon that Race showed any interest in. She made a note to plan a few happy trips for them, New York, maybe onboard a fine ship to London or Spain. They could travel as husband

and wife and no one would ever know. Race suggested that Paris might make a real wedding trip if she would only agree to marry him.

"Why would you want to marry me?" she asked. "I give you my body and my heart freely."

"And what do I give you, girly. A broken down cowboy and a bit of money."

"And your heart and your body, and a warm place to sleep."

"You have a warm place in town." He pulled her closer and she wrapped her arms and legs around him like a vine.

"I have a house. You're what makes this bed warm."

"You know what I think we need to do this summer?" he asked, brushing her hair from her face. "We need a build a fine house here on the ranch. A proper house with polished floors and some of that fine wallpaper we looked at for the saloon. Anything you want."

"I just want to share it with you." She kissed him soundly pressing her breast against him.

March 15th 1881

Race has spent little time in town for weeks. The new house is being constructed and he is more determined to make it perfect than he was the saloon. I love that he asks me about everything and he even took Bella out to oversee the building of the kitchen. He tells me constantly that he wants me to marry him and become the woman of the house. I know he only wants the best for me, but after all I have done I cannot burden him with a wife he won't be proud of.

But I can and do love him....

The house looked like a log castle looking over the valley below. The yards filled with cattle and the shed with tools. There was a bunkhouse that slept ten hands and two guest houses where permanent workers with families could live. It was slowly becoming a working ranch. Race's enthusiasm for the house grew as the stock grew. He was officially back in the cattle business and he was excited about it.

He got stock bulls from Texas and started breeding his own foundation cows. He was looking forward to at least a half dozen calves that would be worth hundreds in breeding stock. The general stock numbered into the hundreds and he was running more in every week, to deliver to the US Army, and the slaughterhouses of Chicago.

Breeding mares were brought in to join Old Jasper's harem and a spring of new colts, each more beautiful than the last was born, and each was worth more than the last.

He was making money almost as fast as Maggie was making money at the saloon. In the midst of it, Race got a letter that had him grumbling under his breath and cursing for no reason.

Maggie brought him a basket of fried chicken and Bella's potato salad, and apple crisp for his lunch. He was still mumbling about the letter and finally let Maggie have a look at it.

My Dear Uncle Race,
I find we have fallen on hard times here. My wife, Delia and I are having powerful trouble feeding four young ones. It

pains me to ask for charity but Delia and I are hoping to travel to Colorado and take jobs in the area. In the meanwhile, we would be happy to work for you for room and board.

It is not in our nature to ask for a handout but we are terrible desperate. We are both hard workers, with strong backs, even the little ones are good at garden work and can handle chickens.

We wait for your reply.

Sincerely, your nephew,

Clyde Garrett

"He's my sister's youngest boy. I never had much time for him. If he's a hard worker, it must be a recent development. I remember him as singularly lazy, sullen and rude to boot. He gave his poor mama a devil of time."

"Maybe marriage has changed him?"

He reached out and gave her rear end a pat. "The love of a good woman can change a man's heart but I'm not sure it'll make a man a worker."

"No, but I bet feeding babies he loves would." She sat the plate of food on the table for him and poured him a tall glass of cold milk.

"You think I should invite them here?"

"He's family. Do you have a choice?"

"We always have a choice. He might be my sister's kid but he has never been kin to me."

She kissed his temple and opened a napkin on his lap. "Do what you think is right."

Maggie knew she was being just a little hypocritecal. She had a sister, and a mother out there in the world and she had done nothing to contact them in months. Maybe it was time to reach out to them and make amends?

That night she sat at her table sharing a drink with Senator Haggen and Judge Bentz. The place was quiet on a rainy Tuesday and many of the regulars were content to drink at the bar or lose money to Cat at the Faro Table. Maggie had a bundle of fine stationary she ordered from New York. The watermark and fine weave marked it as expensive and as she ran her hand over the smooth surface of the velum.

How far she had come. She was no longer a starving teacher writing on crude black boards with broken bits of chalk. She was a successful business woman writing on precious paper, finely crafted with a flowery M.M. printed on the top. It was the sort of thing she dreamed about.

She began the letter to her mother.

Dear Mama,

I hope this letter finds you well. I have moved from Oglala NB to a small town in Colorado. My partner Race King and I have built a new saloon and are making a wonderful living. I am encouraged by our success. My customers include some of the most important people in the region.

I think of you often and miss our Sunday dinners.

I am sending you a bank note for $100. I hope that you will take it as a wish that your life be more comfortable.

With much love and respect,

Your Maggie.

Three weeks later the letter was returned unopened. Maggie tried not to let it discourage her. She wrote a new letter, this time to her sister, Grace. She asked after her and her husband before broaching the subject of their mother. Was she well, and was she still living in New Philadelphia? Then she included the check and asked Grace to pass the money along to her mother.

Two weeks later a reply came addressed to Maggie from Chicago IL.

Dear Sister,

I am glad to hear you are well and happy in the Wild West. Mother is well and living with us here in the big city. A friend of my husband was recently in Boulder on business and saw you in your... work place. Mother does not wish to keep a connection to you because of your lifestyle. My husband is going to run for city council in the near future and cannot risk the exposure a connection to you would doubtless cause.

Please do not contact us directly. If you wish to contribute to Momma's care please send all bank drafts to...

Maggie crumbled the paper and tossed it into her wastebasket.

Bella cocked a brow. "Bad news?"

"No," Maggie said with a huff. "Nothing new at all."

The housekeeper glanced at the envelope and clucked her tongue. "Family can find your heart and break it, no matter how high a wall you hide it behind."

"It that what I do?" Maggie asked. She was busy paying bills and making out her payroll for the week.

"Sure you do." Bella said with a laugh. "Why else would you keep a good man like Mister King at arm's length? You're afraid that he's gonna break your heart like that no-account Cajun." She pretended to spit on the floor.

Maggie rolled her eyes. "So you have me all figured out."

"Yes-um I do. You ain't that hard."

"Aren't. You aren't that hard."

"Well, you aren't," Bella said.

Maggie didn't answer that but she did think about it.

Did she do that, even unconsciously? Was she holding Race away because of Jackson? She was an intelligent woman, in love with a man she knew she could count on. They spent nearly all their time together. His friends and acquaintances were her friends and acquaintances. She knew that there were little or no people in his life who would hold her business against her.

So why did she not agree to marry him?

She turned to look at Bella and smiled. "You're a wise ole' soul. I should pay you more."

"I'm a wise old soul," Bella corrected. "And you should you pay me more."

April 1st 1881

Spring on the ranch meant a flurry of activity. Race's nephew Clyde and his family arrived and have settled in to one of the houses for the hands. It's fun to have children run-

ning around. They are a joy to watch....

Race closed the door on the horse stable just as Maggie was getting out of the wagon. She had changed out of her fancy work dress and had put on her plain brown skirt, boots and hat.

"There's my girl," he said catching her as she slid out of her buckboard. She had brought home dinner for the two of them from the house. Race pulled the bags out of the wagon and kissed her on the mouth. "You're home early tonight."

"It was slow and I wanted to spend the evening with you." She waved to Delia on the porch of their smaller house and for just a second caught a look on Clyde's face that was pure rage. He grabbed one of the children and pushed her into the house and snapped something to his wife that Maggie and his uncle couldn't hear. Delia ducked into the house and Maggie wondered if he was mean to her often.

"Your nephew looks like he swallowed a bug."

"He got a bug in his ear today."

"What?"

"I gave him a couple of chores today while the boys and I were up on the bluff. Got back here and nothing was done. Not a thing. I warned him. His wife and kids are working but I'm expecting a day's work outta him too. I told him get his ass moving or get his ass gone."

Maggie raised a brow at his angry tone. "He has you all riled up."

"Well, I like Delia and the kids are good little kids. But that boy is just plain lazy."

Maggie sat the bags on the long harvest table in the new kitchen and unpacked their dinner.

"I got us Bella's beef stew, fresh bread and a chocolate cake with chocolate icing."

"Chocolate?"

"She got a tin of cocoa powder. You'd've thought I bought her a mink coat."

He sat in the big chair near the small kitchen fireplace and Maggie came to him. He groaned as she began to knead his shoulders between her hands. She could feel the tension in his corded muscles and a little frisson of worry began to snake its way through her.

She rubbed his shoulders until she felt him begin to relax, then heated his dinner and set the table.

They talked through dinner about things that didn't matter, but by the time they were finished Race seemed more relaxed and was smiling at Maggie's stories about the events at the house. By the time she pulled the new white satin nightgown she ordered from a Paris couturiere from her bag, Race was soaking in the big brass tub of steaming water. Maggie stripped off her clothes and stood in front of him twisting her hair into a knot on her head before, she slid into the water with him.

"Well, what's this about?" he said as she slid her wet body against his.

"It's about how much I love you." She grazed his jaw with a kiss and pressed herself against him. The hot water seemed to sensitize her skin making everywhere he touched her pulse. She crawled onto his lap, straddling him in the sudsy water. Maggie used the thick wash cloth to trickle water over his shoulders. She moved to his chest and down his stomach until she slipped the rag around his hardening member. She slowly rubbed the cloth up and down his swelling shaft.

"My God, you are so beautiful."

He groaned and pulled her up, positioning her over his ready cock. Maggie braced her hands on the sides of the tub and sighed as she lowered herself onto his erection. He ran his hands up her sides, the hot water sluiced from his hands as he cupped her breasts. He leaned in and took the tip of one breast into his mouth. He nipped the tender flesh and she shivered and pulled him closer. He kissed her breast, licking the tender flesh, making her shiver. He suckled each tip and urged her to begin to move. Maggie rocked forward and back, dragging a moan from her partner.

"You like that?" she asked, lifting herself up a fraction of an inch. She bore down again and rocked her hips fasted. She could feel him beginning to tense but the faster she moved the tighter her body grew, pushing her closer to her own release.

He kissed her deeply. And Maggie lowered herself tightly against him, rocking harder until she felt him shudder with the power of his release. She rocked forward, sliding herself up his body and let go her tight internal muscles. The feel of his mouth on her breast sent a quiver through her. The power of her climax shot through her, making her arch her back, and screamed his name.

She almost immediately collapsed on him, breathing heavy, her body quivered with the strength of her climax. She wasn't sure she would be able to stand anytime soon. But Race moved her off him and cuddled her at his side until the water began to chill. He climbed out of the water and Maggie watched him dry off that long lanky frame of his. When he was finished he took a new towel and lifted her from the tub, wrapping her in the thick cotton.

Maggie loved the way he cared for her, as if she were delicate, fragile, anything but the tough madam she had turned herself into. He carefully dried her body, his own body growing hard as he tended to her. When he was done he parted her legs and kneeling parted her damp curls and kissed the wet folds of her womanhood. He licked and suckled her flesh, dragging his tongue over her clitoris, making her buck and gasp. He manipulated her flesh until she clutched the quilt in her fist and orgasmed, shouting his name.

Maggie caught her breath and let her heart stop hammering in her breast before she slid down the front of him and took Race's swollen member greedily into her mouth. She drew him in and out of her mouth, cupping his testicles. Massaging them between her hands until Race groaned and pulled her to his mouth. He kissed her deeply, taking a position between her legs and thrust himself into her willing body. It took very little time only a few deep pushes brought them both to a shuddering climax.

They lay quietly in each other's arms. Maggie drifted to sleep and woke to find Race gently brushing the hair from her face.

"I thought you were sleeping?" she said, stretching like a cat against his warm body.

He smiled at her. "I was, but I'd rather watch you sleep."

"Are you hungry?" She started to rise from the bed but he stopped her.

"I can wait 'til morning. I'd rather snuggle here with you."

He must have gotten up to put some wood on the fire because it crackled cheerfully as she cuddled back against him. "I could stay like this forever."

"Well, you know how you can have this forever?"

"How's that?" she asked, knowing the answer already.

"Marry me."

She leaned back and looked up at him. "Okay."

He stopped and looked down at her. "Okay?"

"Okay!"

He took hold of her shoulders. "Are you serious?"

She smiled at him. "I am serious."

He jumped from the bed naked as the day he was born and danced around the room, whooping like a wild Indian. Maggie laughed as he twirled around. After a few minutes, he leapt onto the bed and kissed her soundly.

"You can't take it back, you know?" he said with a laugh.

"I know. I won't be taking anything back. You're right. I wanna be your wife." He kissed her again and pulled her against him.

"I'm so happy, and I am going to make you so happy too."

"You already make me happy, Race. You don't have to do anything."

Race held her close and nuzzled her neck. "We'll get married in New York City, and then take a nice slow ship to Paris, France."

Maggie jumped. "Paris? Really?"

"Nothing but the best for Mrs. Race King."

She snuggled closer. "I love you so much. How soon can we do it?"

"I gotta go down to Texas and bring a herd of Longhorns up the Goodnight and Loving Trail at the end of the month."

"So soon?"

"Sooner the better. I got a friend Matthew Greer. He's running cattle out of Aberdeen. He's selling me bulls at a wonderful rate and I need to add that robust blood line to my stock."

"Can't you wait until after we get back from Paris?"

"No. I need to get all those horny bulls busy on my cows as soon as I can."

"Well, far be it for me to get in the way of a bull's satisfaction."

She didn't want to argue but her heart didn't want to wait that long. She settled in against his warm body and slept a deep dreamless sleep.

The rest of the month flew by. Race took her to the lawyer to see her name put on everything including the ranch, and to the dressmaker for appropriate clothes for a European trip. Maggie felt like a real bride. The girls insisted on having a shower for her at the saloon when Race left for Texas. While she was a long way from a blushing virginal bride, she knew the girls were looking forward to it. Soiled Doves had very few chances to enjoy the sort of things honest women did and Maggie hadn't the heart to keep them from a party like this one.

As Race prepared for the trip south, packing a few necessities into a bedroll, Maggie watched him with a heavy heart.

"Now, how am I supposed to go off and leave you

looking so sad?"

"You're not," she said honestly. "I hate that you're going away. I'm going to miss you so much."

He rolled the pack and tied a leather throng around both ends. He stopped and cupped her cheek with his calloused hand. "I'm going to miss you too, darlin' girl. But do me a favor. Keep an eye on Clyde and his bunch."

"Isn't Clyde going with you?" she asked

Race barked a laugh. "Pushing cattle is hard work and Clyde is the last man I need in the thick of it."

"So what do you want me to do?"

"I know you're staying in town while I'm gone but maybe you can come and check on the place. I told Clyde he don't need to bother with the house but I don't trust him not to come in and out. This is our home. He has no business nosing around."

"I'll take good care of it for you."

She slept in his arms that night and watched him ride away with a dozen of his best men the next morning. As she turned her wagon to the road, she saw Clyde watching her from the porch of the little house and a shiver snaked down her back.

May18th 1881

I miss Race with every breath I take. I received a telegraph that he arrived in Aberdeen and will be leaving soon to bring the herd of nearly a thousand cattle back. It will take him just over five months. A half a year is too long to miss my dear Race....

Maggie did her best to stay busy. She worked at the

house, slept in her beautiful room there, alone and missing Race more than she had ever missed anyone in her life. It was nice to be surrounded by so many friendly faces; the girls were tickled to have their boss around every night. Catherine was making a killing each night on the Faro table. She even pulled Maggie aside to ask her about the possibly of moving on and opening her own house. Maggie hated to see her go but was thrilled that she was doing so well. The house too was raking in money. Word of the house was growing among the population of over three thousand and the City of Denver just a little over twenty miles to the southeast. A determined man could make the ride in less than an hour, and Denver was filled with determined men.

Bella was happy to have her mistress around more, and the two women renewed their fast friendship. Through the days, Maggie oversaw the complete cleaning of the house and saloon. New curtains and linens were ordered and some fancy alcohols and champagnes were added to the list. The place sparkled like a new diamond.

She also waited for the occasional telegraph from Race, telling her about their progress and reminding her that he loved her. Maggie would carry the notes with her as she moved through her day, and reread them at night, so she would dream of his arms at night. She dreamt of his kisses and caresses, his hands moving over her skin, touching her body until she felt heated and restless in her sleep. She woke feeling tense and restless only to fall back into a fitful sleep.

Occasionally the memories of his lovemaking were so real it brought her to shuddering climaxes in her sleep. She dragged out of her bed in the morning tired and frustrated that no amount of cool water could wash away and even her own hands on her skin became a painful reminder of what Race could make her body do.

And through the day she felt down and depressed; Bella would send her off for clothes fittings or to pick up another of the gifts that seemed to arrive regularly from Race.

Maggie's trousseau was nearly complete as the trip entered its third month and August's heat pressed into the rugged mountains. The mines and cattle industry were bringing in lines of men with deep pockets wanting to spend the night with the Silver Filly's beautiful proprietress. She would smile and twist the sparkly diamond ring on the ring finger of her left hand. Race had sent it to her from a jeweler in Dallas. She artfully directed the men and their money to Opal or Cat, promising them a night to remember.

Maggie had no interest in any other man, no matter the money they offered her. She had been looking for a place for herself and found it in Race King.

But the house was not her life. It was her work but not her life. Her life was a thousand miles away driving cattle north. That thought made her giggle.

"What you snickering at over there?" Bella asked. Maggie started to correct her English and Bella raised a hand. "I know, what *are* you snickering at over there."

"I was just thinking about the idea of me driving cattle with Race." Maggie laughed.

"Nothing funny about that. You're the sort of woman that can do about anything you set your mind to, even running cows," Bella said.

Maggie stopped writing numbers in her ledger and looked at her housekeeper. "Thank you, Bella. That's about the nicest thing anyone ever said to me." She caught her hand and gave it a squeeze.

Bella never stopped folding Maggie's delicate lace chemise as she talked. "Don't run on so. I mean it. You're a strong woman. That kind of strong can do anything."

"I don't feel strong without Race."

Bella did stop and gave her a hard look. "You know that no one can make you strong. You make you strong. It's like the way I talk, you can point out my bad grammar but I got to make the change. You got a man who loves you, and that love gives you a reason to be strong, but the strength comes from inside you."

Maggie sighed. "I know and before I met Race I was working on being a stronger, independent woman. But loving him makes me want to be stronger for him."

Bella put a hand on her arm and gave it a squeeze. "That's an admirable thing."

When Maggie and Bella went down to the saloon that evening, the girls had decorated for a party, hanging streamers from the overhead beams and brightly colored gauze that caught the breeze from the ceiling fans. All to celebrate Maggie and Race's coming wedding. And the girls were not the only ones to go all out. Men, several of whom had begged Maggie for a place in her bed, had arrived with small gifts. The governor had sent a box with a beautiful handmade shawl. The mayor of Denver, who Race had supported in his election, sent a painting of a cattle drive. Maggie joked that the cowboy sitting tall in the saddle looked like Race.

Opal and Cassie brought out a cake that Bella had helped the girls bake and everyone at the saloon got a slice and toasted the happy couple with whatever they were drinking. Maggie wished Race could have seen how many people were excited for them.

As the evening was winding down, the girls were beginning to go back to work when the front doors opened and a familiar face appeared.

Harry Boater stood inside the door strangling his hat in his hands. Maggie saw him and for a second her heart slammed into her chest. Harry was with Race and if he was here, Race was here. The cowhand looked tired and covered with trail dust and dirt.

"Harry?" she said.

"I got to talk to you, Miss Maggie." His voice was strained and his face flushed.

Maggie felt the girls gather closer and Bella put a hand to her back.

"It's bad, Miss. Real bad," Harry said. "Race is gone."

Maggie took a ragged breathe. Darkness began to close in on her and Maggie let it take her.

Harry took a seat across from Maggie and with the aid of a glass of strong whiskey began to tell her about the last week.

"We were pushing hard, making close to fifteen miles a day. Race was so happy and wanted to get to Fort Collins as quickly as possible. We crossed the Colorado border and pushed north, preparing to cross the Arkansas River east of Los Animas."

Maggie spread her fingers out on the smooth surface of the oak table. Her chest hurt and every breath felt like a fight. She could feel Bella and Catherine gather close, their hands on her shoulders and back, lending her their strength and love, but she felt cold and weak.

"The spring runoff was high and we debated waiting until the water went down. But I took my pony across and while the water was fast, it wasn't as high as we thought. We decided to push on. More than half of the herd was crossed but we had a few calves that Race wanted to lead. He was determined to keep the calves, all good breeders. But one of the little females got caught up in the flow. I saw Race go after her and then I lost sight of him."

"He drowned?" Bella asked softly.

"His horse, old Jasper, came out of the water a few hundred yards down river. We found him about a mile away. We took him to Los Animas and the undertaker there fixed him up a rig. Luke and I brought him to the ranch. We knew he'd want to be there with you." The cowboy reached out and gave her hand a squeeze.

Maggie came to feet. "I need to see him."

Harry stood too. "No, Miss Maggie. I can't allow that. It's been three days and he was busted up pretty bad. He wouldn't want you to see that."

She started toward the door. "But I have to--"

Bella was the one who stopped her. "No ma'am. You ain't doing that. Mr. Boater's right. Mr. King wouldn't want you upsetting yourself more then you are. You let the men handle this. Miss Catherine, you go fetch her cloak and Mr. Boater, you take us to the ranch. We'll do right by this dear man."

Maggie let herself be moved from place to place like a rag doll. She was empty, hollow as a dead tree and all she wanted was to crawl into the fine oak coffin and sleep next to Race. Bella marshaled the burial like a Union general, and no one, not even the hardest cowboy put up a fight. She slept in the big bed with an arm around her mistress, as Maggie cried herself to sleep.

As the sun came up all the girls, dressed like a murder of crows, gathered at the ranch. Catherine had brought Maggie a simple bombazine dress with a heavy black cloak and hat. Bella washed her, and dressed her in her widow's weeds, and led her to the grave the men had dug on the hillside overlooking the beautiful kingdom he had built to share with her.

The Governor and the Mayor arrived with groups of solemn men. The minister of the Episcopal Church came with his white robes and worn bible to pray for Race's soul. Maggie watched the box that held everything she loved being lowered into the ground and felt her heart die in her chest. At some point she looked across the casket and saw Race's nephew looking at her. There was no kindness in his eyes and after a long moment he looked away. Beside him Delia sniffled into a clean white handkerchief.

"Ashes to ashes and dust to dust." The minister closed his book and offered them to come to the ranch for a meal and time of fellowship but Maggie stood like a statue while they lowered the coffin and two of the young farm hands began to shovel black dirt into the grave. Each hollow shovelful echoed in her heart, and Maggie wished she were dead.

When it was done she walked to the house and ignoring the crowd climbed the stairs and crawled into the bed she had shared with Race.

August 4th 1881

I wonder if it is possible to live without a heart? I feel like a dead woman forced to go on without the will or desire to keep going. I miss him every moment of every day, but find that the world will not leave me alone. I have an enemy and he is determined to destroy what is left of me....

The papers arrived at the ranch by currier just before noon three weeks after Race was buried. Maggie had not yet brought herself to go back to the Silver Filly, relying on Catherine to keep the place up and running. Bella watched her like a hawk as Maggie opened the heavy envelope and began to read.

"Is that Mr. Race's will?"

"No," Maggie said softly. "It's a notice of eviction."

"A what?"

"It seems that Clyde has gotten some judge to void Race's will. He is Race's nearest family and according to this judge, his rightful heir." Maggie felt like someone had kicked her. "I have twenty four hours to leave and not take anything with me."

"That can't be right? How can he do that?"

"I guess because I wasn't Race's wife?"

Bella threw her dishtowel across the kitchen and stomped to the door and shouted for Luke. "Get Miss Maggie's wagon ready," she barked. "You need to go see that lawyer fella that made Mr. King's will. He didn't want that no good nephew taking nothing from you."

Maggie did as Bella said and as Luke drove her to town, her anger began to mount. She didn't care about his money or the ranch, but Race had built that house for her to share with him. She was going to be his wife and if she had to leave she would never lie in the rich black earth beside him, never share his bed again.

Mason Brill looked over the papers and rubbed his chin. He was a regular of Opal's and he had helped Race purchase the land and write his will. He made a grunting sound and rounded the desk to sit on the edge in front of the chair where Maggie waited.

"Clyde Garrett is claiming moral turpitude."

Maggie took a deep breath and let it out in a hiss. "He's calling me a whore."

"He is claiming that his uncle had fallen under the spell of a wanton woman, who influenced him to her benefit and the exclusion of his rightly heirs."

"The only reason Race allowed them on the property in the first place was because I reminded him that they were his family," Maggie said.

"I think we can find enough people to testify to what you and Race meant to each other to have this overthrown," the lawyer offered. "People from the bar. Certainly, you won't get any support from the Governor or the Mayor."

"No. I won't let Clyde drag our names through the mud, or portray Race as some feeble minded..." She sprang to her feet. "Can I have the bed we shared?"

"Only if he gives it to you," Mason said. "I can draft a request and see what we can do."

Maggie sent for Bella and swore never to set foot on the ranch again. She found out that most of the men who had been so loyal to Race had packed up and left. By the time the sun came up again Clyde had a huge ranch, a thousand head of cattle and three men to manage it.

Maggie didn't care about any of it. Her heart was gone, smashed beyond anything it had been when Race was alive. She retreated to the house, suddenly grateful that Clyde had not made a claim on it as well. She felt lost and for the first time since she left Ohio, utterly rudderless.

August 25th, 1881

I find myself swaying between despair and fury. I want to run, to hide, to stop being myself long enough to feel something other than grief and fear. I want to be the "me" I was when Race loved me....

After more than a month, she was able to dress for the evening and join her girls in the saloon. She found her gaze roaming over the poker tables where Race liked to spend his evenings. The crowds were as large as ever and she was surprised to find Catherine in her usual seat, while Callie ran the Faro Table. Cat explained that she had taught Callie the game to give her time to oversee the saloon in Maggie's absence.

"I know you're not worried about this but the house is doing fabulous." Cat reported as she poured Maggie a glass of champagne.

"You're the one doing fabulously," Maggie said smiling at her oldest friend. "Do you want to buy the house?"

The words had come out of her mouth before she even knew she was thinking it.

Catherine nearly choked on her drink. "What?"

"Do you want to buy the Silver Filly from me?"

"You don't want to sell her do you?"

Maggie tried not to look sad. "Honey, I can't have

what I want. But I've been here less than an hour and I still expect to see him every time I look up. I hear the argument we had over the plaster walls, and see the first fire we built in the fireplace. He is everywhere here and it's breaking my heart all over again."

Catherine chewed her lip and looked around the room. Maggie could see she loved the place for what it was, a beautiful saloon, not what painful memories it held. She deserved the Silver Filly and the Filly deserved her.

"What would you do?" Cat asked.

"I have a tent. I can go somewhere, anywhere that doesn't make me want to cry all the time."

Mason Brill sat with the two women the next week and they hammered out an agreement. Catherine secured a loan from the local banker, one of her frequent clients, and agreed to pay Maggie thirty thousand dollars and a share of the profits for two years. Considering what the house was bringing in, she would have it paid off in a very short time. It would give Maggie time to find a new town and build herself a new place, one that was not filled with her heartbreak.

September 1st 1881

Our little band of merry travelers leaves today. We've chosen a small town in the mountains, rich in silver and men lonely for company. It feels so good to be going and good to be looking forward again....

The tent was loaded on the back of the wagon. Harry Boater waited on Race's horse, Old Jasper, while

Luke and two of Race's other hands readied the luggage and mounted their horses. They had all agreed to hire on for the trip. Maggie suspected that they would return to cattle or maybe start their own silver mining operation. Unfortunately, Clyde deceitful move had cut them out of Race's will as well. And because they had backed Maggie, they were never paid for the last cattle drive.

Maggie saw to it they got their wages and smiled when Harry admitted to stealing Old Jasper.

Bella kept the boys working as Maggie got ready to say her goodbyes to Cat and the girls.

Fat tears ran down Catherine's cheeks as she hugged Maggie tight. "Where are you going?"

"Sinners Creek. It's small but it's growing and I want to be a part of that."

Catherine swiped at her tears. "I'll take good care of her. I'll have a plaque made as a memorial for Mr. King and for you."

"Just be happy and make yourself a lot of money. They can't take money away from you," Maggie heard the hardness I her voice and so did Cat.

Her friend took her arm and led her away from the others. "Are you going to be okay? Really."

"Oh really? No." Maggie laughed. "Yes. I'll be fine. But I let my heart lead me into Jackson's bed, and then into loving Race. I can't keep following it off cliffs. I have to follow my head."

"You head can get you hurt too."

"But not so hurt that there's no coming back." Maggie took her head.

"Come back... when your heart is not so hurt." Cat kissed her and Maggie climbed into the wagon next to

Bella.

Harry and the others rode to the side of the wagon and Maggie waved over her shoulder as they started off. She might come back, if her heart stopped hurting but for now there was only one direction she could go.

Forward.

Part Three

No Looking Back

June 17th 1883

I woke with a headache that morning but things turned brighter as the afternoon wore on and news that my new dress was ready at Hattie Dunkirk's dress shop was sent to the saloon. It was red with dyed fur and feathers and a low-cut neckline. But even that wasn't the best part of the day...

The dust of the street swirled around her ankles as Maggie made her way back from the dressmaker's shop. There were few people on the street, mostly men, and all of them tipped a hat or sketched a bow, and a few bade her good morning. The two or three women who passed did so in silence. She was used to that. For two years, she had worked hard as the sole proprietress of The King's Inn. One didn't become the most celebrated madam in Sinners Creek, Colorado without angering a few women.

Not that the majority of the women of Sinners Creek were going to line up to be friends with a saloon owner who offered the kind of extra services Maggie did. There was the minister's wife and the banker's wife, a handful of rancher's wives and daughters, and the new school teacher, none of whom were exactly showing up to welcome her. The irony that Maggie had started out as a school teacher was never lost on her.

But they looked at her with a combination of distain and fear that was only natural, and Maggie respected that distance, never over-stepping her boundaries, in short, never giving them a reason to rise up against her.

The truth was, their anger always made her smile. "Successful people make enemies, buttercup," her father had said. She had enemies and she was damned successful.

John McGregor had known a thing or two about success. He had run a prosperous farm and bred horses that he sold all over the country. He had married well and sired two daughters who were intended for the more genteel life as the wives of gentlemen farmers, but fate had not been kind. Her father had died deep in debt. Her mother had sold off nearly everything, turned her life over to God, and let her daughter to fare for themselves.

Jackson Bajoliere had taught her to make a man weak, to bring him to his knees and make him willing to give her anything to get what he wanted. And he had let her learn to run a successful business.

Race King had taught her about success, to be fair and generous with the people who worked for you and to guard against those who would take advantage.

They had all had a hand in leading Maggie to her current success.

Two well-heeled gentlemen paused on the new plank walkway and smiled broadly. "Morning, Miss Maggie," one of them said as he reached out to help her step onto the sidewalk.

She gave him her most beguiling smile. She would do well to see them later at the saloon and, if their pockets were as deep as their leers, her girls would be happy to leave them panting.

"Gentlemen, beautiful day, don't you think?"

"Indeed," one of them said, casting an admiring eye on her clinging day dress.

Maggie took a deep breath, offering an enticing view of the swell of her breasts over the edge of her neckline. "And it's going to be a wonderful night at the Inn. I hope I'll see you both there."

They both agreed they be there and she smiled as she walked on.

In front of the general store, she stopped and glanced in the window of the Oliver Brady's law office across the street. He was watching her. She dropped her chin and looked up at him from under the brim of her hat. He liked coy looks and she could feel him growing hard, just watching her walk. He would certainly be knocking on her door tonight.

Oliver was her only client at the moment. One of the benefits of being the owner and madam was she got to pick and choose who shared her bed. And while it was necessary to keep at least one man in the hook for an income, her reputation let her choose from some of the finest men in the territory.

There was no doubt about it, Margaret McGregor was a Sinners Creek success story, and she was damned proud of it. She had rolled into town driving a wagon overflowing with girls, booze, and a tent she had won in a poker game, and a heart so wounded that the desolate little town of Sinners Creek. There had been little or no town to speak of. A few hastily put up buildings that offered a place to drink an overpriced beer and measure out the day's earnings in chunks of shining rock were all the town could boast. But Maggie's eye for business had seen more. The town was like her, a little rough around the edges, a little sad, dusty and impatient for more, but both were willing to work to make things better.

And she certainly had.

But the King's Inn was not like the Silver Filly.

Gone was the flashy, showy side that Race had given her leave to follow. It was a nice place but when the Governor came visiting, he did so under cover of night and only because the Lady of the house had invited him to her bed. It was a working man's bar, in a town were even the men with the money were hard workers.

She offered fair prices for beer and a steady supply of harder liquor, and even a little champagne when a miner wanted to do up a celebration right. A cook who could handle pots and pans and produce a home-cooked meal was added, along with a bath house with a row of shiny cooper tubs. Hot water was extra. And of course, there were the girls.

Maggie still offered a passel of the prettiest girls west of the Big Muddy. Natural blondes, brunettes, even a redhead whose crotch was as fiery as her locks. Girls who were ready, willing and able to sell a man a poke or a few other more imaginative services for the right price. She even had a pair of sisters who were willing to take a man on together for double the fee and a healthy tip.

Her girls were among the best, a far cry from the crib girls who hawked their tails on the streets and used themselves up in a few short years.

Some of the girls were so exception that some of them were married and moved on to lives far different from the saloon.

And the men had flocked in, some nights they came from the camps by the wagonload and waited for hours to get one of the girls, and all the time they drank like it was their last day on Earth.

And the money rolled in.

Thinking about Race still made her sad. She missed

him so much, his quick smile, and quiet manner, his strong hands. She missed his soft snoring in the long darkness, the way he reached for her in the night, the way he said her name when he made love to her, as if he were uttering a prayer.

He was the reason she was here, the reason she could put one foot in front of the other and she missed him so much. He would have loved the way she kept going, and that she was a part of a town that was coming up.

She truly wished he could see it.

Now, Sinners Creek had two crossing streets: Main Street and First Street, and few dozen buildings. There was talk of a grand town hall and a large new church was being built at the end of First, ironically some of Maggie's money was going into both projects. She had no use for either politics, or religion, but they were another step on the way to her little town becoming something great.

So she donated to political campaigns, to civic development projects and even municipal beautification works, starting with the raised plank sidewalk that now lined the street from the courthouse, past the assayer's office and her own saloon.

Houses and families would follow, but for now the town was hers.

Maggie climbed the stairs to her private entrance. Her maid, Bella, was waiting.

"Took you long enough," the older woman huffed as she snatched the package from Maggie's hands. "I need to get this frock aired out if you wanna wear it tonight."

"I think I'll save the new one for Saturday." Maggie

said, shrugging off her short jacket and handing it to her maid. Bella had been born a slave but she earned a fair wage working for Maggie. It was the same for Maggie's working girls, and she saw to it they could read, write and play the piano as well. It was the least she could give them for the hard work they gave her. "I'll just need the white robe and the lace underclothes for tonight.

"Silk and lace? That mean the lawyer gonna be here this evening?"

"If I'm any judge," Maggie said stepping into her private quarters.

"He's gonna want dinner and a bath too."

"He does like the way I scrub his back."

Bella said with another huff, "I'll tell Mary to fry some chicken. I ain't polishing his boots this time. He can take it to that boy in front of the bank, if he wants shiny boots. How long did he go this time without getting his knob polished?"

"Nearly three weeks," Maggie pulled the blinds to darken the room.

The large black woman looked back and grinned. "You might wanna get a nap, you gonna need your strength."

Maggie took the suggestion, waking just after six and stepped into a warm bath. Bella was right about one thing, when Oliver came through that door, no power in heaven or earth was going to get in his way. He had been visiting her for nearly two years, but in the last few weeks he had been talking about marriage and family. Not with her; no one expected a whore to marry and produce children. He would go back east and find a suitable girl to wed and bed, one who would be a proper wife for a judge or a senator or what ever Oliver decided to become next.

But he always came back to her eventually. He would smile and flatter and beg her to spread her legs. She would give in after making him suffer a while for making her wait so long.

Maggie didn't really mind. He was richer than Midas, handsome as sin and hung like a horse. No reason to resist that.

She toweled dry and dressed in a thin chemise and drawers. She threw on a white robe and belted it. Bella began to fill the tub with hot water and laid out fresh linens for her guest. The clock had just struck ten when the door opened and Oliver's face appeared in the doorframe.

He smiled broadly and handed her a bunch of field flowers.

"How charming," Maggie handed them to Bella. "Put them in some vinegar for me, would you?"

"Now Maggie," he said, letting Bella take his hat and coat too.

"You ignore me for nearly a month and I'm supposed to welcome you with open arms? The hell with you, Oliver Brady."

"I got you a hot meal and a warm bath waiting," Bella said. "You make yourself ta home, mister."

Dinner was brought along with buckets of hot water and Bella left them alone to get to business.

"So what will this cost me?" he asked. "An arm, a leg?"

"Nothing so personal." She began to undo the pearl studs on his shirt front.

"The usual?" he asked, running a hand up her satin-covered arm.

"Double," she whispered.

He raised a dark eyebrow and pursed his shapely lips. "It better be worth it."

She slipped her right hand into his shirt and brushed a nipple with her nails. Her left hand dropped to the growing bulge in his trousers. She cupped the heated flesh separated from her hand by only a thin layer of wool.

He groaned softly and pressed her mouth to his to catch the sounds. "You know I am worth every penny," she breathed against his mouth.

"I know that, beautiful."

"Slip out of those clothes and I'll get that French soap you like so much."

He was out of his clothes in less time than it took her to get the sweet smelling soap bar out of her cupboard. He slid his naked body into the water and watched as she crossed the room to join him. She took a soft rag and dipped it into the water. She worked the rag around the soap and the scent of Bay Rum filled the air.

Maggie brushed the lather over his shoulders and down his spine letting it briefly brush the small of his back before bringing her hand up to circle around his shoulders again. He leaned back against the copper tub and watched as she swirled the rag over his chest and lower over his stomach. She shrugged out of her robe and her breasts pushed against the fabric of her silk chemise. She dropped the rag into the water but continued to rub her soapy hands lower. She felt the muscles of his flat stomach contact. Lower still and she took his swollen member into her grasp. He was a nice sized man in all ways. His perfectly proportioned body was always a pleasure to pleasure. His long muscled arms and legs, his strong broad chest, his flat stomach and nearly foot long manhood made her mouth water.

It was almost a shame to charge him, but she did anyway.

Maggie continued to run her hands over his body, carefully touching, arousing every inch of him, just the way he liked it. Her simple silk chemise got wet and clung to her plump breasts, just the way he liked. He reached out and touched a nipple under the damp fabric and she sighed, just the way he liked.

When his dick began to throb, he stood and the sight of it made her smile. She reached for the soft cotton towel and began to dry him off, he stepped from the tub and the water clinging to his body ran down her skin. He was more than ready, and so was she.

The damp fabric clung to her skin and the warm moisture began to pool between her legs. There had been a handful of men in her bed in the last six years, since she traded her virginity for an education, some she believed she loved, some she truly adored, but this man was one she just enjoyed. The heat between her legs became unbearable. The tissues in her secret folds began to throb with need.

He liked that too.

Oliver liked that this beautiful, wonton, lusty woman wanted him as much as he wanted her, and the none-too-gentle prodding of his engorged member against her soft flesh was proof he wanted her.

Now, to give him everything he wanted.

Maggie licked her lips and kissed his mouth, catching his lip between her teeth and sucked it into her mouth. She kissed his strong jaw and down his neck. She ran her tongue along his collarbone. She took a pebbled nipple into her mouth and laved it with her tongue.

Oliver pulled the pins from her hair and ran his fingers through it, shaking out the dark wavy tresses. She knew he liked to take her hair down, to watch it fall against his skin as she tasted him. He wove his hands into the thick locks and gently guided her head down his front. She let him move her but took the time to run her mouth over his stomach and lick at his navel. Lower, she rubbed her cheek against the coarse hair that arrowed a path from his belly to the thatch where his pride waited for her.

Maggie moved her hands down his back to his buttocks and gripped the muscles. She got onto her knees in front of him and looked up at him. His gaze was as hot as fire as he looked down at her.

This moment meant everything. He felt big, he felt powerful with this small beautiful woman about to pleasure him in the most intimate way possible. But Maggie knew the truth. She was the one in control. She might be on her knees but she could bring him to his in a matter of seconds.

Maggie smiled coyly up at him, and licked her lips and opened her mouth. She kissed the tip of his penis and his eyes rolled back into his head for a second. He recovered quickly, because he did not want to miss seeing what she did next. She closed her mouth over his shaft and quickly sucked it deep into her throat.

He groaned like a man possessed and he had to

lean back slightly to stay on his feet.

Maggie loved that moment. Many of her girls hated to practice fellatio on their customers. Maggie didn't agree with that at all. She loved it. It gave her power, control over her clients. She could make them come quickly or drag out the pleasure as long as she liked.

Oliver would go for hours and she would play him like a fiddle.

She let her lower teeth grate the underside of his dick, the *vaisseau sanguine*, Jackson had taught her about so long ago, and his knees nearly buckled. She let the wet member slip from between her lips and flicked her tongue over the tip again. She did this over and over until he started to grip her hair. He was getting close and she didn't want to waste that moment. She stopped her play and he held out a hand as she got to her feet. She led him to her bed and as he sprawled backward on her silk counterpane, he smiled that wickedly handsome smile.

"I missed you, beautiful."

Maggie huffed. "Missed parts of me, I'm sure."

She lifted the wet Chemise over her head giving him full view of her pump breasts. He licked his lips and sucked in a breath over his teeth. "Looks like they missed me too."

The room was cool and damp cloth had made her nipples pucker. She let him think it was just him. It never hurt to salve a man's ego and a man like Oliver had a lot to be egotistical about. She looped her thumbs into the waist band of her silk drawers. Pulling them slowly down her long legs. She bent at the waist and shifting her hips slightly to show off the curve of her backside. He loved her backside and she loved watching his prick stiffen again as she unhooked the silk stocking from her garter. She rolled them down and off one at a time, as he watched her with feverish eyes and that muscle between his legs stood fully erect, the tip of it turning deep red.

"I'd say part of you missed me a lot."

Fully naked, Maggie stretched like a cat and slid one leg onto the bed.

"It did indeed," he said reaching out to run a hand along her hip. She planted her arms on either side of him and slid her body close to his.

Maggie put her hand on his calf and slowly drew it up his leg, wrapping her small hand around his large dick. She tightened her fingers gently around the shaft and released it, repeating the motion until he closed his beautiful blue eyes and leaned back against the stack of soft pillows. "You keep that up and you're going to get a hand full of cum."

She leaned down to lick the tip, which was now all but pulsating. "Maybe a mouthful?" she asked playfully.

She knew very well that was what he wanted more than anything. He opened his eyes and fished his hands into her thick hair. "Are you trying to kill me, beautiful?"

"No," she purred and the vibration of her lips still touching his tip made his swallow hard. "I just want to make you happy."

She ran her tongue around his tip then licked the underside to the base. She burrowed her lips into the damp thatch of hair and kissed the sensitive underside of his balls. He jumped like he had been burned with a flame.

She continued back up, rubbing the length of him against her cheek and purring again like a cat in heat.

"You want me to taste you?"

"God, yes. Please beautiful."

"You know it's gonna cost you?" she said and her tongue did a swift dance over his tip.

"Anything," he begged.

"Take me riding tomorrow."

"I'll ride you now," he ground out the words, but didn't move.

"Promise," the pout her lips formed molded over him and he groaned.

"Anything, beautiful, anything."

Maggie smiled and opened her mouth. He groaned and pushed her head down so that the entire shaft of his dick was in her mouth, partly down her throat. She relaxed and let him go.

Years ago, Maggie learned there was a difference between giving a man a blow job and letting a man fuck your mouth. She was very particular about that difference. Not many men got to hold onto her hair and force himself in and out of her mouth the way Oliver did.

This was a privilege she gave him, one he would pay for. In a few short moments she felt him spasm and buck like a wild thing. A second later she felt the hot liquid in her mouth. She took a deep breath and pulled back, taking a silk hanky off the night stand she spit cum into it.

He lay for a while breathing hard, the sweat beads on his nose and forehead spoke to the Herculean task of not shooting his wad faster. He smiled as she daintily wiped her mouth. He liked that too, that he had gotten her to do something she rarely did. He knew she had just done him a favor.

She lay back on the pillow next to him. "So where are you taking me?"

"I'll should take you over my knee and paddle your pretty ass. Making deals with me while your breathing on my cock is hardly playing fair."

"Who said I was playing fair?"

"Where do you want to go, beautiful?"

She twirled a lock of her hair while she hummed softly. "I'll leave that up to you. But it has to be nice and it has to be fun."

"Fun," he said with a laugh. "I can take you to bed, that's fun."

She smiled at him. "I agree but this is a special occasion. Maybe you should take me to Boulder for dinner?"

"Half a day's drive to get a meal." He leaned up on an elbow and teased her nipple.

"You can go to hell," she started to get out of the bed and he pulled her back.

"I promised you something special and you'll get special." He pulled her into his arms and she could feel the heat in his crotch again. A few minutes of pleasant talk and he was ready to go again. "Now, let me give you something special."

He slipped his fingers into the trimmed patch of hair crowning her thighs. She opened her legs and let him dip into the wet folds of her skin. He stroked her flesh pushing deeper into her and making her moan. He found the pulsing bud of her sex and rubbed it until it throbbed. His mouth found hers and kissed her deeply, and moved lower to her neck and then her breast.

He played his tongue over the tight nipple, taking pleasure in the dark want that filled her eyes. He licked and nibbled at her flesh, sucking greedily on one nipple, before moving to the other.

The delicious tightness began to build in Maggie, it would be easy to let go and release the pent up desire thrumming through her. But she wanted more than his hand. And she wanted him to come again.

She pushed him away slightly and turned to her left, with a few small movements his hard shaft was pressed to her fleshy bottom.

Oliver growled and pulled her waist hard, bending her slightly and taking position behind her. Maggie spread her legs and reached between them to guide his hot cock into her. When he was there, she straightened up and gripped the metal headboard of the bed. He used his knees to spread her legs wider and pushed hard into her. In a heartbeat, he was hammering into her making her breasts bounce and her head sway. She could feel him deep inside her. He slipped his hand around her hip and into her vulva again. He found her clitoris and stroked it hard. He rocked into her again and again until they both exploded with passion.

He wrapped a hand around her and held her as their bodies throbbed together.

June 18th 1883

I woke up so happy this morning, for the first time in longer than I can remember. Like a little girl at Christmas…

Maggie hated morning, she always felt sore and tired and, with other men, often frustrated as hell. But morning with Oliver was a pleasant thing. Because he was a single man, it was easy for Oliver to stay the night, and mount her hard again in the morning. He always woke her by parting her legs and climbing between them taking her hard and fast.

Maggie would wake to him breathing hard, calling her beautiful and telling her he had to have her again. And she woke up horny as hell when he was there. She wanted him in her, wanted him to kiss her breasts and taste her skin. He pumped her hard, each deep dive into her body dragging his cock over her throbbing clitoris and making her scream his name as she came. The added wetness made him slip easier and come faster.

By the time he left her bed, Maggie was as sated as he was.

Bella stepped into the room when Oliver left, and the scent of coffee and bacon followed. Good thing too, since Maggie was starving. The housekeeper set her plate on the table and oversaw the filling of the big copper tub with steaming hot water. After eating hardily, Maggie slipped into the bath. The hot water caressed her skin and soothed her muscles, she settled in with a sigh. One of the best things about Oliver was she never had to pleasure herself after he was done with her. She just relaxed and tried to imagine where he was going to take her for their special day.

Maggie was dressed in her finest blue traveling dress, and grabbed a matching parasol as she walked to the second floor common room to talk to the girls before she headed out. As she passed Mabel Strams' room she heard the bed frame squeal and the sound of groans. It was just little after nine A.M. and Mabel was making money. She needed to remember to have Harry, the bartender and general handyman grease Mable's bed springs.

In the salon, Aggy, Garring and Helen Broom were sitting down to breakfast with the Dellard Sisters and Alice Breck as Maggie stepped in.

"Oh, someone is going out this morning." Alice said, taking in Maggie's dress.

"I am," Maggie gave Augusta a pat on the shoulder. "Aggy, can you take care of the house for me until I return?"

Aggy smiled up at her. "Of course."

"The beer deliveryman will be here this afternoon, Harry will pay him, but he usually wants a visit upstairs. Can you entertain him?"

"Happy to," she said, returning to her breakfast.

"The men from the overland express will be here around dinner time. They will all be randy as goats. Divvy them up however you all like. If Amos Lathy shows his face around here, call the sheriff. I should be back tonight or tomorrow at the latest."

"Is that good lookin' lawyer taking you somewhere special?" Amy Dellard asked with a knowing smile.

"I certainly hope so."

The afternoon was bright as a new penny as Maggie stepped out the saloon door. The Brewster Brougham sat in the street with the curtains pulled closed. Maggie hesitated on the sidewalk glaring at the box. Jonah Isaacs sat on the driver's seat smiling. Oliver had hired the coach and the driver from the livery to hide himself away.

"He said you'd be mad as a wet hen." Jonah shot a wad of tobacco spit into the street and handed her a single red rose. "He said give you this, and for you to get your pretty butt in the carriage, ma'am."

Maggie took it from Jonah's hand. The door opened and she joined Oliver in the closed brougham. "Are you ashamed of me or something?"

"Never, but I do have to be careful. I want to run for the senate and--"

"You think you're the first senator whose pecker I've rubbed?"

He smiled. "No, I know old Willis Dawes still comes knocking on your door when he can."

"And he still sends me a birthday present every year."

"He thinks highly of you," Oliver agreed. "But I don't have the luxury of the whole state thinking of me as a kindly uncle."

"So am I going to hide in this dark carriage all day?" she asked with a pout.

He helped her settle into her seat and pulled a bottle of champagne and two glasses from a basket on the floor. "I promised you a special day and special is what you'll get."

The road was rutted, but the champagne was cold and the company was good as they rode away from the boomtown they both called home. She waited until they were well away from town before she pushed open the curtains and let in the fresh air and sunshine.

There was something special about the valleys around the high Rockies. It was all so different from where she had grown up near New Philadelphia, Ohio. And maybe that was the point. She had wanted to get as far from home as she could and this was certainly it. She hadn't minded moving around but this was the sort of place a person could stay, get lost in and be content in.

The carriage rolled to a stop much sooner than she expected. And, as he promised, Oliver opened the door and stepped out, then reached in to help her down. Maggie had no idea where she was. A long stretch of valley dipped between lush rolling hills, with the towering Rockies in the background. A grove of trees clustered to her right and a wide creek flowed out of the mountains and raced away out the valley in the distance. It was beautiful.

"Very nice," she said. "There is nothing here."

He laughed and the sound of his voice echoed down the valley. "You would think that way."

Oliver went to the carriage and took out a large bundle and the picnic basket. Maggie waited, enjoying the bright sunlight and the rising temperature. He came back as the carriage began to roll away.

"Where is he going?"

"To give us a little privacy. Come this way."

"A picnic? That is my special day?" she asked.

"You sound unimpressed. You who spend all your time working or planning, and I wanted you to have one day to relax."

"In nature?" she said doubtfully.

"In the only thing that rivals your beauty." He took her hand a led her to the side of the creek. He put out the thick quilt and basket and helped her take a seat. "See? Perfect."

Maggie smiled at that. It was beautiful and she did find herself relaxing into her special day. He poured her more champagne, and took packages of cold chicken and beans. She watched him do something he never

133

did in the past. He waited on her. She took off her bonnet and jacket and opened the throat of her blouse. She even took off her boots and stockings.

They ate and chatted like friends. Oliver laughed when she took off her skirt and waded into the cool water.

"You really do have a hard time keeping your clothes on," he said and she pointed out that his jacket and boots had been discarded for some time.

"Are you having fun, beautiful?" he asked.

Maggie smiled at him. The water was warm and she decided to really enjoy it. She unbuttoned her top and tossed is onto the quilt, her chemise and petticoat joined it. She shook out her hair and settled into the cool water naked as the day she was born.

In a matter of moments, the water rippled and a very naked Oliver joined her. He gathered her onto his knee and she could feel his warm flesh even in the cool water. Her back was pressed against the hard wall of his chest. He brushed her hair to one side and kissed the pale column of her neck, nibbling the soft flesh and running his tongue over the pulse point under her ear.

He breathed his want and desire into every whisper. She felt herself growing warmer. The cool water did nothing to stop the heat that began to build between her legs. That part of her wanted his touch, his need, his talent wanted more than just a leisurely dip in a stream.

Maggie reached beneath her and found his hardening dick. Oh, how she loved the feel of it against her skin, in her hand, under her power. She rubbed him until he was hard as the rocks beneath them. She lifted herself and slid his dick into her. She rolled her buttocks backward and heard him gasp. She tilted her hips forward and he groaned. She rocked back and forth like riding a big horse, slowly moving him in and out of her wonton flesh. It felt so good having his thick hard cock inside her and his long elegant fingers finding the folds in the front. He parted her wider, abrading the delicate flower of her sex. She began to move fast, pumped harder, rode him deeper into her. His other hand came out of the water and found her breast, he gathered the plump globe and gently kneaded it, then brushed his thumb over her hard nipple.

She bucked and wriggled pushing herself tighter into his lap, onto his throbbing dick.

"You like that?" he whispered.

"Oh, yes," she said and tossed her head back. She wanted it and so much more.

"I'm gonna make you come, beautiful," he said with a wicked laugh.

"Yes, Oliver," she said riding him back and forth. "I wanna come on you."

He bounced her a little while longer then plucked at the bud and Maggie gasped, pumping hard, taking him deeper as her muscles tightened around him. Oliver pumped up into her, joining her in her thundering orgasm.

They rested on the bank of the creek, waist deep in the clear cool water. Slowly, they toyed with each other's bodies. A kiss, a touch, a finger ran along and over sensitive nerves, until their heartbeats slowed and their breath became less labored.

"That was special," she said, kissing his jawline.

"Yes it was." He took her hand and helped her up.

After a few slippery moments, they were standing naked in the sunshine. "But that was not the reason I brought you here."

She leaned against his side let him drape his arm over her shoulders.

"You see this valley? From the top of one hill to the top of the other as far as the eye can see, is yours."

She hesitated for a minute, unsure what it was he was saying. "Mine? How is it mine?"

"I bought it for you." He pulled her close, pressing her breasts against him and kissed the top of her head.

"Am I going into ranching?" she asked with a laugh.

"You can go into anything you like, beautiful."

It took her a full minute to understand what he was saying to her.

"It's mine?" she said, turning to take in the broad sweep of the valley and the little hills that hemmed it in. "You bought it for me?"

"Yep, every inch of it."

She hugged him tight. "No one has ever given me anything so grand, not without a huge price attached."

"There are no strings attached to this." He tipped her face up to look into her eyes. "There was a time when I didn't have a friend in this world but you, beautiful. Now, I have a chance at everything I've ever wanted. That's in no small part because of you. You introduced me to the right people and made a few connections for me. I want to do something for you."

"But this?" Her gaze traveled over the tall weeds and wild flowers.

"Now before you get too excited: this is no land for raising cattle and the ground is good, though I don't picture you farming it."

She laughed. "You make it sound worthless."

He hugged her tight to his side. "That it is not. You just own it, and let me do the rest."

She was overjoyed. Their relationship had always been the same, sex and money. But this was more than that, more a gesture of friendship, and admiration. She let out a squeal and leaped into Oliver's arms, she wrapped her legs around his waist, pressing her muff against him. He stumbled backward landing on his back on the soft quilt. She wasted no time slipping a hand between them and cupping his growing erection.

"I'm going to wear you out, Mr. Oliver Brady, Esquire."

She crawled down his body taking his growing rod into her greedy mouth. She licked and sucked and moaned, rubbing his heavy balls between her hands and working him until he was hard and hot and ready for her.

She slid up his body again and straddled his groin, jamming his dick into her hard and fast. She pumped him hard, rubbing her heated breasts against his skin. He pushed her away only far enough to gather her soft breasts and bury his face in them. He licked and sucked her nipples as hard as she had his cock. She took him deeper, pumping him harder and groaned as he did the same to her nipple, drawing it into his mouth hard.

In no time at all he hammered up into her and she felt him pulse inside her. She tossed her head and orgasmed with a cry of joy.

The sun was setting and they were cleaned, rested and dressed as they climbed into the carriage for the drive home. She knew it would take about an hour to get back to Sinners Creek and a lot less than that to say thank you. She ran a hand over his thigh and into his crouch.

He smiled at her. "Haven't you had enough?"

"I don't need anything after today," she said undoing the buttons of her blouse. She had left off the chemise. She parted his legs and lowered herself between them, laying open her top for him to play with her breasts. He toyed with her while she undid the buttons of his fly and took out his limp dick, she fingered and kissed him until he was hard again she took him between her breast, stroking him with the pale mounds.

His eyes burned as she rubbed the crown of his dick over her nipples.

"My god, beautiful, is there nothing you can't do to me?"

She smoothed her hands over him as she lowered herself and took him into her mouth. She sucked him deep, taking him hard and fast, stopping only to blow a hot breath over his wet cock. She did it over and over until he came into her mouth.

She was wiping her mouth when she joined him on the seat where he leaned panting in the corner.

"Thank you, Oliver," she said softly and carefully tucked him into his pants before buttoning them up.

June 19th 1883

If this is all a dream I hope I never wake. Oliver has changed my life and I can't begin to thank him...

The next day, she got a note asking her to drop by

his office for a chat and to dress conservatively. That part made her laugh. She wondered if he was intent on bending her over his desk and fucking her right there. She didn't mind that so much, but it did make her nervous going into his office. She wasn't use to socializing with her clients, and she never, ever considered visiting their workplaces. She was a prostitute, not a friend, and certainly not the sort of person most people, even her roughest customers, wanted dropping around for a chat.

But that was exactly what Oliver's note had said... "Beautiful, stop by my office at ten A.M. for a chat and please dress conservatively." She hoped her gloves covered the tremble in her fingers as she opened the door and stepped into the offices of Weiss and Brady, Attorneys at Law on the other side of Main Street.

In the outer office a young man sat with his eyes agog as she came through the door.

"I'm, Miss--"

"I know exactly who you are Miss McGregor. Mr. Brady is waiting for you," he said, standing to open the door for her. She stepped into the well-appointed room and found Oliver deep in conversation with an extremely well-dressed man. Both gentlemen came to their feet and greeted her with broad smiles.

"Ah, here is the woman of the hour," Oliver said, reaching out to guide Maggie into the office. "Margaret McGregor, let me introduce you to Victor Anderson. Victor, this is our Maggie."

The stranger took her hand and bowed over it, and pressed a quick kiss to her gloved knuckles. "It's a pleasure to meet you, though I am a bit at a loss as to the reason for our meeting."

"Your very clever lawyer here tells me that you are the owner of a particularly large particle of land north of the Comanche Peak area?"

Maggie took the seat Oliver held for her. "I am." She looked up at Oliver for confirmation.

"And I understand you purchased it with no particular purpose in mind?"

Maggie smiled. Purpose? She had no idea she'd had it until the day before. "No, sir. I have no particular plans for that land."

The two men exchanged a smile and for a minute Maggie thought she might have been set up for some kind of joke. Then he took out a large paper and unrolled it on Oliver's desk.

"I work for the Denver Pacific Railroad and we would like to purchase that tract of land," he said, a smile making the corners of his eyes crinkle. "My company is taking a new set of rails west into the Montana Territory, and as it happens, we need to purchase that piece of property from you."

Maggie wasn't certain what she should say. Oliver had only just given her that ground. But there had been something odd about the way he talked about it. He had said it wasn't good for much, and that he didn't see her as a farmer or rancher. Was this what he wanted all along?

She looked at Oliver for some sort of guidance. He smiled broadly and raised his eyebrows.

"I'm prepared to make you a very rich woman."

Suddenly it all made such wonderful sense to her. He had to have known that the railroad was coming, that this piece of ground was right in the path of progress.

There were few things in the world that made Maggie blush, but there was something about the way Victor Anderson was smiling at her that spoke to her. There was kindness in his eyes, mingled with desire, and something that made Maggie return the smile. She felt like she had just been let in on a joke, one that was bound to tickle even her untouchable little heart.

Everyone was making money on the railroads, and a growing number of men coming into her house were attached to the great iron horse. There was no reason to think that she couldn't or even shouldn't be one of the multitude making money.

"Well, I have always wanted to be a very rich woman, Mr. Anderson, or can I call you Victor?"

Now, it was his turn to blush, "By all means, please call me Victor."

Oliver was watching them both with a smile on his mouth, which surprised Maggie. He was never one to share his toys. He insisted on her undivided attention, so this was different. Not that Maggie cared. He didn't own her, no man had since Race King died had that kind of claim on her, and that was exactly how she intended to keep it.

The papers were signed and a breathtakingly large bank draft was turned over to Maggie. Just like that, a lifetime of struggle and sacrifice was over. It was more than she could make in a lifetime on her back.

Mr. Anderson asked if he could call on her in the future, and Maggie agreed with a coy smile. And she and Oliver were alone in his beautifully appointed office.

"You planned this all along, didn't you?" she asked as he rounded his desk and took a seat on the leather swivel chair he had shipped in from Boston.

"I met Victor on the train my last trip East. He had a few stories to tell about the railroad and the new lines to Montana. I saw no reason that a little money couldn't be made."

"A little money!" she all but shouted and waved the check from a New York City Bank. "Did you see this bank note?"

Maggie walked to the door and flipped the lock, then crossed to the window where she drew down the fancy French blinds. As she walked back to Oliver's desk she pulled the pins in her hair and shook it loose. Oliver smiled as she began to unbutton her jacket.

"I'm working, Maggie," he said with no conviction.

"I'm saying thank you," she said, hanging her jacket on the back of a chair. She took her time unbuttoning her blouse and laying it with her jacket.

"I have a lot to do today." His eyes took on a feral gleam as he watched her round the desk and come lean against it. She untied the strings of her silk chemise and opened it to bare her breasts. He fondled her as she leaned down to undo his belt. She undid the buttons of his fly and felt him growing beneath the fabric. She pulled the wool back to expose his growing cock.

"I only have one thing to do today," she said lifting her skirt to reveal no petticoat or bloomers.

"You came into a meeting wearing nothing under your skirt?" he said with a laugh and ran a hand up her naked thigh.

"My meetings usually include what I have under my skirt. I thought this might too. You said conservatively not like a school teacher." She undid a tie at her waist and her full skirt came away falling to the floor.

His eyes focused on the crux of her thighs, and the trimmed thatch of hair crowning her womanhood. He ran his hands over her hips as she settled onto his lap near his erection. She closed her hands over his shaft and drew her hands up the length of him. He groaned and leaned back in his chair giving her more room to play with him. She interlaced her fingers around him creating a tight cup of her hands. She ran her thumbs over the tip of his penis, catching the droplets of jism and using them to lubricate her hands as she moved it up and down his shaft.

"God, beautiful, that feels so good."

"I can make you feel even better," she said leaning in to kiss him hard.

She pumped him hard, bringing him close to orgasm and then slowed to keep him from coming. Over and over she brought him to the brink and denied him release. He began to squirm, kneading the soft flesh of her thighs. He slid his right hand up and his fingers found her cunny. He spread his knees, which widened her spread legs and exposed her even more. He slid into her find the hot wet folds. He slid two fingers deeply into her and pressed the heel of his hand against her opening.

His other hand found her breast, swaying seductively in front of him. He tweaked a nipple, making her breath catch in her throat.

She continued to pump her hands, bringing him closer and he gently thumped his palm against her clitoris and buried his fingers into her. Finally, together they reached the pinnacle and slammed into exotic ecstasy.

Before he could melt in her hand, she slid forward

and pressed his cock into her. She wriggled tight against him, taking him deep before he lost his erection. He kissed her, running his tongue into her mouth, brushing sensuously against hers, drawing it into his mouth to suck on it.

He moved down her neck and brushed the tip of her luscious breast with his tongue.

"You drive me crazy, beautiful," he said then sucked her nipple into his mouth.

She wove her fingers into thick dark hair and rocked her hips against him. She tightened her internal muscles around him and felt him respond. "I want to drive you into me."

He growled and taking her with him stood. He laid her back on the desk and drove himself into her. She bucked and wriggled and pumped her hips, meeting each hard thrust with a tilt of her hips and a groan of delight. He rammed harder, and she groaned deeper, her breast dancing up and down like a Cancan girl. He caught them and squeezed gently, hammering deeper until she tossed back her head and tightened around him and he let go, pumping her hard with his climax.

She propped herself on her elbows and looked over her nearly naked body at him as he collapsed back into his chair.

"No more, Maggie, Please."

She giggled and threw a leg over him to stand. The truth was it was no easy task. She felt heavy and sore and spent, and happier than she had in years. He did up his pants and watched her dress without leaving his chair. When she was all bundled up and her hair piled careful back on her head with pins holding it in place, he smiled and held out a hand.

Instead of his lap he handed her to the chair next to him.

"I want to talk about what happened here today."

"The part where you made me a rich woman or the part where I thanked you?"

"The land deal." She nodded and listened intently as he leaned forward and lowered his voice. "Victor Anderson is a very powerful man, Maggie. He wants you, and he always gets what he wants."

"Isn't that the way of most men?" she asked.

He thought for a moment and smiled. "I suppose that is the truth."

"I feel like you're trying to warn me about something, Oliver but I'm a big girl and more than able to take care of myself." She came to her feet and Oliver took her hand for a second.

"I never doubted that."

He stood and walked her to the door. In the waiting room, a small blonde-haired woman was sitting in one of the oak chairs, toying with the string of her handbag. The clerk looked nearly apoplectic at his seat behind his desk. Everyone stood as Maggie and Oliver stepped out of the office.

"Mary Grace?" Oliver said. His voice, slightly higher pitched than usual, made Maggie notice the woman even more.

She was very pretty in a soft, delicate way. Her blonde hair was piled carefully on her head and her dress was expensively made but not garish. She carried a parasol made of lace and decorated with embroidered flowers. She had an air of old money about her, but there was a bright intelligence in her eyes.

"Mary Grace this is one of my clients, Margaret

McGregor. This is Mary Grace Shaffer, my fianceé."

Maggie did her best not to react. She smiled at the small woman and extended a hand.

"You own The Kind's Inn Saloon?"

"Yes, I do."

"But you're so much younger than I thought you'd be. I admire any woman who can operate a thriving business all alone."

Miss Shaffer took her hand and gave it a squeeze, her smile never faltered from her face and Maggie thought she would make the perfect politician's wife. If there was any part of her that didn't want to like the woman, it was that she was going to be Oliver's wife and wives always spoiled her fun. But she didn't think she could dislike her at all. She seemed very genuine.

Perhaps she would be less complimentary if she had witnessed Maggie riding her fiancé like a bucking bronco ten minutes earlier? But she hadn't and Maggie would have bet the check in her hand bag that this innocent young woman would not think such a thing even possible.

"Well, thank you. Mr. Brady. Thank you for handling this agreement for me. Miss Shaffer, it was lovely meeting you. And congratulations on your engagement."

"Good afternoon." They both said as Maggie turned to the door and escaped to the bright street.

June 19th 1883

Oliver introduced me to Victor Anderson and again my life has taken an unimagined twist. I also met Miss Shaffer. Oliver will marry her and I will be fine…

Maggie sat at her table, her reading glasses on her nose, and toyed with her account books. She had stopped by the bank and deposited the check.

Fifty-thousand-dollars.

The young man in the teller's cage had taken the check back to Old Mr. Tallmadge who immediately came out of his office and greeted her enthusiastically; something the old man had never done in the past. But then she was a very rich woman now. It would no doubt change a lot of people's attitudes toward her.

On the other hand, meeting Oliver's future wife with his cum still wet on her thighs had been a shock, even to a woman not easily surprised. She had known that he would marry, but she hadn't known he had met anyone. And she hadn't expected to ever meet his wife-to-be.

She focused on the account book and the numbers in the income column. It really was amazing and she was happy to spread a little of it around. She was working on a list of things to get for the girls when a light tap on the door brought her gaze up from the paper. "Yes?"

The door opened and Oliver put his head in. For moment she wasn't sure what to say to him. He stepped in and she closed the book on the table.

"Maggie." He looked uncertain and she nearly laughed. He was never uncertain.

"What can I do for you?"

"I want to explain." He put his hat on the rack and crossed the room to stand near the table.

Maggie took off her glasses and watched him move closer. "You already explained about the land and the deal that was too good to pass up. Or do you want to explain to me that you are getting hitched?"

"I owe you that." He took a seat and reached for her hands but suddenly that seemed too intimate. They weren't friends. She was reminded of that today. She stood and moved away from him.

"You don't owe me anything, Oliver, any more than I owe you. We have a delightful arrangement. I've been more than compensated for that arrangement. Nothing more."

His eyes were growing flinty in his handsome face. "I want to explain."

"I'm a grown woman, and I've been in this business long enough to understand how things work," she assured.

"Well, I haven't been in the business very long and I need to explain."

"You want to be Senator Brady and you'll need the right wife for that. Miss Shaffer looks rather perfect for the part."

"Her father is a powerful man in Washington politics and — "

"I'm happy that you've found someone to help you get what you want."

"But I do care about her. She is a lovely person."

Maggie turned to look at him. He didn't sound like himself. He was always so sure of himself, always so confident.

"Who are you trying to convince, me or you?" She circled the table and stood behind him. "I've met her. She's lovely and I'm sure she will be an excellent wife and she will probably produce a lot of beautiful children. Now, you tell me what this all has to do with me, and why it warrants this little visit?"

"I'm not just marrying her for show. I want her to be my wife."

Maggie smiled at that. "She looked eager to take on the job. Are you trying to say you won't be coming around to see me anymore?"

He didn't say anything to that.

"You'll be an excellent husband, Oliver, and a great senator."

"That was really the reason I wanted to introduce you to Victor. He has all the information on the railroad, where the rails are going and what land is going to be purchased next. He can make you more money than you ever need.

"Are you taking care of me?" she asked.

He reached out and cupped her cheek. "I don't want you to have to keep working if you don't want to."

"But I like my work." She ran a hand down his chest and over the mound in his pants. "And I'm good at it."

He smiled at her and ran an appreciative hand over the lace covered bodice of her dress. "That you are, beautiful."

She began to slowly undo the buttons on the front of her dress. "So you're going to wed that fine young woman and give up coming to see wicked old me. In the meanwhile you've made it so I never have to mount a man again, unless it's purely for pleasure's sake, of course."

"Of course," he said taking in the sight of the mounds of her plump white breasts.

"So can I mount you, one last time, for pleasure's

sake?"

He leaned in and kissed her hard. She could taste whiskey on his breath and wondered if he had needed a glass to fortify him for this little speech to her. They weren't friends, but she was fond of him, and she would miss not having him ignore her for weeks then come around with a massive erection and money in his hand.

Maggie stepped out of her dress and taking the pins from her hair, shook it loose. Oliver slipped a thumb under the straps of her chemise and edged it off her shoulders freeing her breasts for his exploration. He kissed a hot trail over her flesh, taking the puckering nipple into his mouth and sucking hard on it. She tipped back her head pressing her body closer and pulled her arms from the fabric.

As he lavished each breast with attention, she loosened her ties and undid her buttons until the dress and petticoats fell to a heap on the floor. The ribbon at the waist of her drawers was next and they too slid off her body. Oliver ran his hands down her sides to her hips and stepped back so she could kick the assorted garments away. She was naked and Oliver stood back to take in the sight of her.

He would miss her, she knew that by the way he fought out of his jacket and shirt, by the way his skin prickled when she ran her hands appreciatively over his pecs, brushing the taut pap with her nails. He bucked and shivered and fumbled with buttons on his trouser.

And she would miss him, miss the fun and the sweet care he took in seeing her pleasured as much as he was. She would miss the way his eyes darkened as they roamed over her body. And she would miss the searing heat that coursed through her when he filled her and rode her body to a hard climax.

But more than that she would miss the way he made her laugh and the gentle sweet way he spoke to her. His quiet respect for what was normally a disrespectful connection. She would miss Oliver Brady, and watching his star rise with his loving wife at his side, would be harder than she wanted to imagine.

She had been very lucky, for a soiled dove. She had known some brutal, careless men in her days but she had also known men filled with great kindness and generosity too. She had seen the worst of men as many women had, but she had seen the best of them too. This was one of the best and she wanted this last time to be special.

Oliver finally tossed the last of his clothes into the pile with hers. He was always so careful with his city man's garb, seeing him kick them aside made her laugh.

"Your suit will wrinkle," she said softly into his ear.

He pulled back from kissing her neck and smiled. "I'm not at all concerned about my suit. The only thing on my mind is this beautiful woman in my arms."

He lifted her into his arms and placed her on the bed, taking her mouth in a deeply soul searing kiss. He kissed her temple and jaw, down the column of her neck, where her heartbeat echoed just under her tingling skin. Oliver carefully nibbled her shoulder and her upper arm. At her elbow he kissed the tender inside of the joint, sending a ripple of excitement down her spine.

Oliver was always thorough. It was as important that she have an orgasm as his was. That, in and of itself, made him different from most men, but this time was special. He was taking his time, pleasuring her slowly.

Maggie knew he was saying goodbye.

If that was the case, she would let him, and make him hard as a rock to boot.

He moved to her breast again, licking and kissing the rounded globes, taking the pebbled nipple into his mouth greedily. Maggie leaned back on the bed enjoying the attention and slipped her foot between his thighs brushing his swollen manhood with the ball of her foot. He bucked at the unexpected contact and smiled up at her.

"Tricky?"

She giggled and ran her hands through his thick hair.

He kissed a trail down her body, over her ribs and the soft plane of her stomach and before she realized what he intended he had slipped her legs over his broad shoulders and settled between her thighs. He blew a puff of breath into tidy curls on her mound and spread her knees wide to open the folds of her womanhood.

Another hot puff of breath and she gasped at the intimacy of it contact. He placed a simple kiss on the folds of her labia and she felt herself melt into the touch.

She had gotten very good at giving a man pleasure with her mouth but rarely was a man willing to do the same for her. Oliver slid his tongue into her, licking the wetness pooled there, and then ran his tongue up and over her clitoris. She opened her mouth but only a groan escaped her lips.

He burrowed his tongue into her flesh. Maggie gripped the sheets as he flicked his tongue over her bud, sending shockwaves of pleasure through her, waves of hunger crashed into her and it was all she could do to keep from falling right off the bed.

When she orgasmed it was like a cannon had gone off inside her. The feeling rumbled through her and she let out a cry of pleasure and wove her fingers into Oliver's dark hair as she bucked against his mouth.

He moved away from her and smiled at her.

"My god, Oliver," she said when she could speak again.

"Pretty amazing, isn't it beautiful?" he said casually wiping her jism from his mouth.

She fumbled for the word.

"Amazing? Fantastic? Incredible?" he offered.

"Yeah." She lay back on the bed and panted until her breath slowed and her heart had stopped hammering against her ribs.

He crawled up her naked body and kissed her. He was so hard, so ready to pleasure her again and this time she was going to give him the ride of his life. She rolled him onto his back and straddled him, guiding his hard cock into her folds and he pushed into her wetness with one hard thrust. She took him deep and rode against his pelvis as hard as she could. Her breasts swayed in front of him tempting him to taste them. He pulled her closer and took her nipple into his mouth sucking it hard. Maggie tipped back her head and gave herself over to the pleasure of it all. Oliver drove up into her harder and faster until he exploded inside her, pushing her to her own peak. She threw back her head and screamed his name.

Maggie lay on her stomach with her eyes closed and tried to let the moment last as long as possible. She knew what was coming next. He was leaving. He had a fiancé, a mother for his children, a partner for his future and he wouldn't need her after today. She would be a pleasant memory that he would remember when he was alone, or when he mounted his little wife.

Maggie didn't want to be jealous. Not that jealousy would get her anywhere. She had been in love, really in love and she couldn't begrudge that for anyone else. But she had learned after Race's death to be realistic about her life and her work. She was paid to make men happy, to give them pleasure and then to go away.

There was always a beginning and an end to her relationships. The beginning was fun and exciting. They gave her money and lavished her with presents and attention. Then, time went by and they came to her with worries and woes. And in the end they were out the door without a backward glance or a thought for her.

Oliver was always very different.

He had charmed her and talked to her. He had given her the gift of independence. But he was leaving and she was going to have to straighten up and go on.

Oliver rolled onto his side and ran a finger down her spine. It made her shiver.

"You were wonderful."

She rolled to face him and that finger traced over her shoulder and down her chest to toy with her breast. This was the thing she was really going to miss. Of all the men she had slept with since Race, and there had been a few, Oliver was the first one that she let get close.

"Thanks you, sir. You were pretty wonderful yourself. When are you leaving?"

He stopped and arched a brow. "I'm going back to the hotel tonight."

"I mean. When are you going to Boulder?" she asked, encouraging him to fill in the details.

He seemed to not know what to say.

"You can't run for senator from little old Sinners Creek." She gathered the sheet and wrapped it around her to cover her body. "And you will be senator, so you need to marry that pretty little girl and get your fine ass to Boulder."

He sat up on the bed and reached for her. "I want you to know that you are important to me."

For just a moment, she lovingly cradled his cheek in her hand. "I know that darling, but you got stuff to do. I will not let you forget who your friends are when you're running this part of the state."

She slipped into her white silk robe and tided the belt shut. Maggie watched him silently as he stepped from her bed. When he was fully dressed, she straightened his tie.

"Do I have your blessing?" he asked taking hold of her shoulders.

"You don't need it. You need my money. And I expect you to help the women of Colorado get the vote."

Oliver kissed her softly and closed the door behind him. Maggie crossed to the windows that looked out over the street behind her building. Oliver stopped on the new wooden sidewalk and lit a cigarette. She could see the red tip of it as he walked toward the hotel.

She took a deep breath and wiped away a tear, then crossed to her desk and picked up the card on the blotter.

Victor Anderson, Vice President of the Denver Pacific Railroad.

She smiled and began to write a letter.

My Dear Mr. Anderson,
I believe you and I can make a great deal of money....

Part Four

Happily Ever After

May 5th 1884

My partnership with Victor Anderson has made me wealthier than I could have ever imagined. I have people around me that I can trust and rely on, but there is still something missing. I am as defined by my life here as I had been defined by being a teacher or a daughter. I long to do the things that Race and I talked about, to travel and see the world, but I'm afraid it will mean nothing without him....

Maggie signed the bank draft and smiled at Mr. Finch at the other side of the desk. The banker was used to dealing with workers and silver miners. Maggie always found him polite and pleasant but he always looked nervous.

"Can you arrange a letter of credit for me?"

"Of course, Miss McGregor. Are you traveling?"

"I'm thinking about it. I love the mountains but there are so many other places that are beautiful too."

"Sinners Creek will miss you."

She patted his cheek and his Adam's apple bobbed convulsively. "I will miss this place too, Mr. Finch. Maybe you can stop by the Inn. You know, Helen is really fond of you."

Maggie returned to The King's Inn and found Bella glaring at a large trunk.

"Is it being contrary?" Maggie asked.

"It's being too small. How'm I supposed to get everything I own in this little trunk?" Bella asked.

Maggie absently folded a lacy dinner shawl she had bought her and which the housekeeper had never worn. "Why are you packing everything? You won't be working on this trip, so don't you pack anything you wouldn't wear to Sunday service."

"What if we never come back?" Bella asked indignantly.

"We'll be back, but if we don't, I'll have someone pack up everything and ship it to you. Now, send Luke down to Tillie's for any of the trunks she has in the shop."

Bella went for Luke and Maggie continued to pack her things. She wanted to see some of the places that she and Race had talked about, New York, London, Paris. Places she had read about in books. She loved her life, loved the girls who worked so hard for her, loved Harry Boater and Luke, and loved Sinners Creek. It had become her home, a place to retreat to... to heal.

But she needed to do something. She needed to talk to people that didn't know everything about her already.

She was wealthy. Her partnership with Victor Anderson had made her more money than she could imagine, more money than she could ever spend in this lifetime. Her goal had been to be independent, to never have to starve or beg, or be beholden to men like Deacon Harris who had taken her virginity in exchange for a teaching degree.

But now she needed to do something, to see something other than the same faces and same places. She needed to be away from everything. So she bought two tickets to New York, ironic on the railroad that her less than honest dealing had helped build, and told Bella to pack her things.

May 29th 1884

Bella and I have bought passage to London on the White Line's ship "The Republic." We leave New York in three days. The trip will be about two weeks, and we will arrive in England in time to enjoy summer in Europe. I believe this will make me happy and if it doesn't, I can be unhappy in a beautiful new place.

The last of the trunks were loaded into the carriers and a steward was assigned to see it delivered to Maggie's suite on the beautiful ship. It had a great stream engine that aided the three great sails that caught the fickle wind. It would take the one hundred and fifty first-class and one thousand steerage passengers safely across the great blue Atlantic Ocean.

Maggie stood on the dock and waited for the steward to lead her and Bella up the gently sloping gangplank. No one here knew her, knew what she had done to earn her first class ticket. They saw a well-dressed, obviously wealthy woman with her maid and they accepted that picture as all there was; a wife joining her husband abroad, or a widow putting her past behind her.

They did not know her, and that was fine by her.

Their cabins were adjoining, a large master room and a smaller room with a comfortable bed. A third room was equipped with a washstand and a familiar copper tub. "All the comforts of home," Bella said, dropping her reticule onto her bed.

Bella had dressed carefully the first night for dinner, but after taking a look at the gentrified look of the first-class dinner hall, she opted to eat in the room. The food was amazing but the company seemed less than friendly as Maggie entered the hall. For just a moment she struggled with the idea of returning to her cabin and eating with Bella. But then, she reminder herself was the object of the trip was to meet different people, and these people were definitely different. There was not a rough neck or cowboy in the bunch.

Her décolletage of her green velvet gown was a bit lower than the other women's necklines, but the shawl—a gift from Governor Willie Dawes—covered her shoulders. She pulled it closer around her as the footman escorted her to her table. She made herself comfortable and did her best to ignore the gazes that followed her. But the whisper of conversation went on around her was distracting. Finally the Captain of the ship, Capt. Adam Graham came and gallantly bowed.

"Is your cabin satisfactory, Miss McGregor?"

"It's lovely. And the ship is very impressive."

"May I invite you to join my party?"

Maggie gave him her hand and let him escort her across the room to his table.

"This is Mr. and Mrs. Simon Markel. Coronel Kennedy. Mr. and Mrs. William Aberson, and Connor Grant, the Earl of Carrick. Ladies and gentlemen, may I introduce Miss Margaret McGregor."

She was seated between Mr. William Aberson and Mr. Simon Markel, but it was the man across the table from her, the handsome Earl of Carrick caught and held her attention.

He was tall and well-built. His blonde hair had been carefully combed back, except for a wayward lock that fell over his brow. His bright blue eyes followed her as she settled into her seat and accepted a glass of wine.

"Are you travelling alone, Miss McGregor?" Mrs. Emily Markel asked, and Maggie watched the woman's gaze taking in the expanse of skin above the green velvet neckline, not surprisingly her husband's attention was on the same place.

"Myself and my personal maid, Bella."

"You're so brave travelling without a male escort," the older woman pointed out, though it sounded more like an accusation than a question.

"I have no male to press into service." Maggie smiled at Mrs. Markel, but her gaze slid to the man across the table, who was watching her closely. "And I really didn't want to wait any longer to see the world."

"What parts of the world do you want to see?" the Captain asked.

"London and Paris, for a start. Then where ever the wind takes me."

The captain smiled and raised his glass. "To where the wind takes us."

Maggie enjoyed her first three evenings aboard ship. She got to know a few of her traveling companions and dined each night with a new group. Her afternoons were spent resting, talking with Emily Markel and watching the endless rolling sea.

There was no dancing, no bawdy songs or men vying for time in her bed. She talked to Mrs. Merkel who was so engrossed in discussing fashion and travel she forgot Maggie's low necklines. And all the while The Earl of Carrick watched her. As the night wore on, Maggie said her goodnights and headed to her room.

At the top of the stairs she noticed the moon shining off the waves beyond the rail of the great ship. She gathered her shawl tighter around her shoulders and stepped out into the chilly night air.

The view was amazing. The waxing moon danced on the tops of the waves and the clouds scuttled across its face, moving her in and out of the shadows. She stepped to the rail and breathed in the salty air.

"Beautiful."

The voice washed over her like warm honey. She turned to find the earl standing a few feet away. The moonlight glinted off his blond hair and the end of his cigar glowed red in the moonlight.

"It is breathtaking, isn't it?"

"I wasn't referring to the moon," he said, stepping forward to join her at the railing.

She smiled at him. "I'd hoped you weren't."

He looked down at her. Those deep blue eyes searched her face. "I admire that American directness."

"I think you'll find I'm a bit more direct than most Americans. You were very quiet at dinner... what do I call you? My Lord? Your Earlness?"

He laughed. "Why don't you call me Connor?"

"Connor. It's a good name. But there must be more to it?"

"Lord Connor Grant, the Sixth Earl of Carrick."

"Impressive," she said with a smile.

"And stuffy. I much prefer Connor. And what do I call her Miss Margaret McGregor?"

She leaned closer and took his cigar from his fingers. "Maggie." She took a deep drag from his cigar and tossed it into the ocean. She wanted his hands free. She squared herself in front of him. "It a pleasure to meet you, Connor."

They talked for a while in the moonlight and Maggie could see that he wanted her, she recognized the way his eyes trailed over her body, the slight sheen of perspiration that shimmered on his smooth brow, the way his tongue moved across his lower lip. He was more than interested in her and she was starting to feel the same.

She wondered if it would shock him if she took him back to her cabin and showed him who she was, who she really was.

"It's chilly out here. Can I get you a drink to warm you?" he asked.

"I would like that. Bourbon. Neat."

He was still smiling broadly when he stepped into the lounge. He returned with two crystal highball glasses with perfect amber liquid in them. He held his glass up and Maggie touched her glass to it. Connor smiled. "In England we don't touch glasses."

"Really? Well, let's play it English then." She held her glass up.

"To new friends," he offered.

"To good friends," she added.

They shared their drink under the gathering stars.

"Where do you call home?" he asked.

"I was born in Ohio. My father was a horse breeder, but I have lived in Colorado for the last five years. I own my own business there."

"Let me guess, a school for young ladies?" he said.

"I was a teacher. A school of sorts. But not a school for young ladies."

He leaned against the railing. "Now, I am intrigued. I'm trying to get a bead on you."

Maggie liked that.

"But I think you want to be a mystery,' he said, sipping his drink.

"What clues do you have so far?"

"You are educated. You have social graces. You obviously have resources."

"I am educated, social, and rich. Yes."

"You are adventurous and fearless."

"Within reason."

"Suddenly, I want to kiss you very much."

She stepped forward and lifted her face, accepting the warm press of his well-formed mouth on hers. She kept the kiss chaste for a moment and then stepped closer, turning her mouth and opening to his sudden plunder. He groaned and invaded her mouth, only to find her a willing and through kisser. She drew his tongue into her mouth and gave as good as she got. After a breathless moment he lifted his head and looked at her with amazement.

"Have I shocked you, my Lord?" she asked.

"No," he said though the look on his face said he was shocked.

"Then, I will have to try harder." She took his hand and led him back to her cabin.

Inside the cabin, he seemed confused as to where to stand. Maggie took off her shawl and found two clean glasses on a buffet. She poured him a drink and helped him out of his coat. 'Would you like to sit and relax?"

He took a seat and sipped his drink while Maggie stepped behind a room divider and began to remove the green dress. It took a moment, and she chatted to the suddenly uneasy Brit as she took off her encumbering clothes and slipped into one of her silken gowns and robes. She had pulled the pins in her hair and was shaking it out as she stepped out from behind the screen.

"I must admit, you have me at a disadvantage, Maggie."

"Connor, you are free to go anytime you like. But I thought we would get to know each other better."

He took off his jacket and pulled off his silk cravat. "I want to get to know you very well, Maggie."

Maggie began to remove the studs of his perfectly fitted dress shirt. She kissed him deeply as she slid her hand into his shirt to brush her fingertips over his nipple. He hurried out of the shirt as Maggie began to unbutton his trousers. She could feel him growing hard and made him gasp as she cupped his heavy crotch, massaging the growing flesh.

He groaned and slipped off her robe and the straps of her silk gown. It slid off her skin with a hiss. She stood naked as the Earl hurried to catch up with her. His pants and underclothes ended up in a heap on the floor.

He was only a few years older than her, not thirty years old yet and his body showed the tone of an active life. He didn't have a work-hardened body, but it was beautiful, nevertheless. She ran her hand through the dusting of golden hair that dipped between his pectorals and down over the flat muscles of his stomach to the thin line of hair which knifed down from his navel to the patch of gold around his erect penis. There she slid her hand along its length and Connor bucked like a stallion.

Maggie smiled. "You like this?"

"More than you could possibly know." He leaned forward and caught her mouth. He captured her face and held it as he claimed her mouth. He pulled her close, slipping his hands through her hair, cupping the back of her head as her bent her backward and plundered her mouth.

The kiss was all consuming.

The kiss deepened further and Maggie felt as though her skin was on fire and every nerve ending was singeing from the heat building in her body. She slid her hand into his hair holding him in the kiss just as he held her. She heard him groan, it was a sound she had heard many times, but this time she felt it, through every part of her body. He broke the kiss and trailed a line of kisses down her neck and over her chest, all the time holding her in strong hands. Maggie had never felt like this, as though she were being feasted upon. . . devoured. . . consumed.

By this time she would have moved them to the bed, begun to touch his body to build his desire but that wasn't happening, Connor was touching her, moving her. His left arm held her up, tight against his mouth as he worked his way lower, finally taking her breast into his hot mouth. His right hand cupped her breast, and then slid down over her belly and between her legs.

Maggie tried to clear her head. She reached out and found his heavy erection. He moved his hips pressing it into her hand and she closed her fingers over him. She began to move her hand up and down the long, hard cock. As she slid to the base she cupped his balls and massaged them between her fingers. Then she slid up the shaft and gave the swollen head a gentle squeeze.

Connor groaned again but if she thought he would be distracted from his task she was wrong. She felt like a rag doll being moved, turned, worked, his fingers didn't hesitate, he parted the damp folds of her skin and delved deep into her body. Now, it was Maggie who bucked and quivered. She didn't want it to stop. He plucked at her womanhood, playing her like a musical instrument until she wanted to sing out.

Connor kept the movement up as he stepped toward the bed and laid her out on the soft coverlet. He continued to suckle her breast, nuzzling her flesh while she held his head to his task. His fingers continued to move over her clitoris; tighter and tighter her body became. Connor kissed a blazing trail over her stomach and followed his fingers into her torrid folds. He licked her, nipped the flesh already pushed to the edge of release and finally delved his tongue deep, still moving his finger over her swollen bud.

Maggie's climax was like a volcano going off in her body. And Connor only delved deeper, pushing her climax on. It extended from a few seconds to wave after rolling wave of pleasure. Maggie gulped air into her lungs as her muscles spasmed with decadent deliverance.

Connor crawled up her body. She had no time to even gather her thoughts before he slid himself into her wet passage. He kissed her deeply, drawing her tongue into his mouth. He began to pump into her, lightly at first and then with a mounting force that kept Maggie from any rational thought. And her body responded. Despite having just experienced the most powerful orgasm of her sexual life, the desire was growing again, the tightness growing. He rode her hard, pushing her relentlessly until she was close to the brink. Connor seemed remarkably in control. He slipped his hand between them and into the place where their bodies seemed forged together.

"Relax, my dear. Let me show you something miraculous."

He gently pinched her flesh and the pressure seemed to ebb, only to come back like a tidal wave when he released the fold of skin. He did this over and over, all the while keeping up the steady rhythm of push and withdraw, push and withdraw.

Finally after what seemed like forever to Maggie, they both came. It was the most powerful thing she had ever experienced. Maggie shouted and clutched at Connor as though she had never had an orgasm. And she hadn't experienced anything like that before.

They collapsed onto the bed, panting like they had just run twenty miles. Maggie was actually a little lightheaded. Connor had crumpled, landing partly on her and partly beside her. Their bodies were still forged together with sweat and passion.

As Maggie began to be able to think clearly, she marveled at the sensations still reeling through her body. Connor pulled her close and stroked her hair as though petting a child. She fell asleep for a moment and woke with a start to find him smiling at her.

"Where did you learn those tricks?" she asked.

"I've traveled extensively, India, Asia, Turkey. I see someone has taught you a thing or two."

"I was engaged to be married once and we were very much in love." It was the truth, not the whole truth but all she was willing to share with him.

"Why did you not marry?"

"He was killed before we could wed."

"I am sorry. You must have loved him very much to forgo the bonds of marriage for intimacy."

"You are very different from most men I have met. I like you."

"Oh, my dear, you have never met anyone like me. And I suspect I have never met anyone like you." He kissed her soundly and crawled out of the bed.

She rose on her side and watched as he dressed. He really had a magnificent body. He was perfect, as though he were carved from flawless marble. "Do you need to leave?"

"Oh yes, despite our new friendship, you are an unmarried young lady and I will not be the one to sully that image."

He kissed her again and finished dressing, then leaned down to kiss her tenderly before opening the door. He looked both ways before slipping out and away. After a few moments, Bella opened the adjoining door.

"You okay?"

Maggie collapsed back onto the bed. "I'm not sure," she said truthfully.

"I was afraid he was killing you."

Maggie laughed and then buried her face in her pillow. It was embarrassing to find herself so out of control.

"How about I fix you a hot bath?"

"Yes, please," Maggie said. Her voice and subsequent giggle were muffled by the linens.

May 30th 1884

My encounter with Lord Connor Grant has left me confused and frustrated. Physically, I have never experienced anything like this stranger's lovemaking but emotionally, I am having real trouble with what I am feeling. I have never been confused about men, but this one baffles me. I am torn between avoiding him entirely and dragging him back to my bed....

Maggie soaked in a hot bath. For several minutes, the muscles and nerve endings of her vulva quivered and pulsed like a thing alive and maybe it was. As her body finally relaxed, he mind began to turn over what she had experienced.

He had taken her over, done things, and touched her in ways she had never been touched. He had learned these tricks not just to bring himself pleasure, but to bring her body pleasure too. It was so all consuming and it left her uncertain.

The seducer had become the seduced. The thought left her rattled.

She had always been in control, from the moment she opened herself to Jackson. She'd known what she was doing, what she wanted. With Jackson she had wanted to learn. To be as good in bed as she could be, to bring a man pleasure, fill him with desire and the need to have her. With her beloved Race it had been to experience real love, to give herself totally to him. With Jackson, Oliver and the others it was to secure her own future, to keep herself safe.

At any time in her life, she could have taken an entirely different path. She had been free to choose what she wanted, who she wanted and where she would go next. Now, very suddenly, she didn't feel in control. And she wasn't sure why.

She spent a fitful night tossing and turning, reliving each touch and even climaxing in her sleep at the power of the memory. She woke to the bright morning sun and a mild headache which left her out of sorts. Bella brought her a light breakfast and a pot of strong coffee, then finally, fixed her a headache powder. Maggie dressed in a warm day dress and long fur-lined cloak and went to the deck to sit in the sunshine.

She dozed and read Mrs. Ward's new novel Miss Bretherton. Emily Markel, who seemed determined to take her under her wing, had stopped by, to invite her to lunch with her and several of the other women of First Class. Maggie had finally agreed, just to get her to leave. She had just gone back to her book when a shadow briefly fell over her and Connor took the seat next to her.

"Good morning, my dear. And it is a lovely morning."

"Good morning, my lord. Did you sleep well?"

"Like a babe. And you?"

"Very well, thank you."

He lowered his hat to shade his eyes from the sun and leaned back, the picture of relaxation. "I was hoping you might join me for lunch, if you are not already engaged."

He was playing the proper suitor, and she would play along. "I have a luncheon date, but my evening is free."

"Dinner and dancing in the ballroom?"

"I'd love to."

He sat a while longer commenting on the sunlight and the seagulls that flocked around the people tossing bits of bread for them. He complimented her cloak and hat.

Maggie smiled at him. "You're trying very hard,

aren't you?"

"I'm sorry, does it show?"

"It's subtle, but then, I'm a suspicious sort."

"I was hoping to impress you," he said, lighting one of the dark cigars he kept in a gold case. The smell of the smoke waft over her, reminding her of home and work and for just a second, who and what she really was.

"You impressed me, Lord Carrick. Have no fear. Tell me about your travels to the Orient."

"I would rather show you," he said, giving her a handsomely wicked smile.

"Oh, that might be part of the lesson, but I am eager to hear about the countries as well."

He talked for a while, perched in the deck chair, about the people he had met and the places he had seen. He talked about riding elephants and eating raw fish, about sleeping under the stars in tea fields and on boats floating on rivers whose names sounded like music.

Then he asked her about her home, the cowboys and Indians, the towering Rocky Mountains and vast grassy prairies, of dance halls and cattle drives. She could see him imagining the frontier with the same awe she dreamed of Asia. After a while, Emily Markel came to fetch her. Connor excused himself and Maggie told Emily to go ahead to the dining room and went to change into her dress for lunch.

"These Brits have more rules about clothes than I ever seen," Bella complained.

"Saw," Maggie corrected, then waved her off. "I know. I'll never keep it all straight."

"Never mind," Bella said. "I'll learn it. I made

friends with Mrs. Markel's lady's maid. It's what you gotta call me you know, your lady's maid."

"I said you were my companion," Maggie said stepping into her dress.

"Well, don't say it again. I'm a proper lady's maid for a proper lady. You got to remember them things."

Maggie looked at her and smiled. "How are you doing? Are you having any fun at all on this trip?"

Bella smoothed the coverlet of Maggie's bed. "Not the kind of fun you're having, but I am having a good time. The food is wonderful and I made a few friends below stairs. That's what they call the help in England, servants, below stairs. But then, being a lady's maid, I'm a servant above stairs. Don't it sound fancy? And you know they never had slaves there?"

"I knew that."

"It's a very interesting place and by the time we get there, we're gonna fit right in."

Maggie loved Bella's excitement. She let Bella fix her hair and hurried to join Emily in the dining room. The older woman was sitting with an assortment of cold finger sandwiches and a plate of pastries. It was all very pretty and so feminine, Maggie found herself carefully sitting on the dainty chair and wishing for bourbon and branch. She was bored, not with the company by the conversation... until Emily mentioned Connor Grant.

"He is very handsome. Too bad about his family." The woman stuffed a small cherry tart into her mouth.

Maggie poured herself a second cup of tea and smiled. "I'm sorry. What about his family."

"Carrick's father was a good man, but a poor business man. The Carrick fortune is nearly gone.

Maggie finished her luncheon and listened to the gossip about Connor and his father's unfortunate penchant for gambling. How Connor had inherited an estate mortgaged to the gills and indebted to nearly every merchant in London and York.

Amazing!

When Maggie thought about what she'd had to go through to get a simple bank loan before her partnership with Victor Anderson.... How could an entire nation with the power of England run with such strange rules?

She entered the dining hall, and immediately the handsome Earl rose to his feet to greet her. He helped her into a chair at a private table. He flashed her a wonderfully wicked smile.

"You look delicious this evening." His voice was provocatively low and flowed over her like warm water.

"So do you," she said with a slight purr in her voice. She wanted him to know she wanted him.

"I have thought about you all day."

"I've thought about you too. In fact your name came up in several conversations."

"Should I be thrilled or horrified?"

"A bit of both." She smiled as the waiter brought them course after course of the evening's meal.

"So you have talked to Mrs. Markel. I can't think she was terribly complimentary."

"They were highly complementary to you, more complimentary than they would be to me should she find the truth of our friendship. I do find it fascinating that my selling sex for money considered a shock and a sin but selling yourself into marriage for money, icluding sex, I might add, is considered par for the course and successful business."

"If it's any consolation," he said lifting his glass. "The la bon ton will never know the truth about us. Your friendship is as dear to me as any I have ever made."

"And if it leads to a pleasant night, all the better." She raised her glass and drank a toast. "To pleasure and friendship."

"Pleasure and friendship," he echoed.

After dinner, they spent two hours on the dance floor, enjoying the conventional contact of one waltz after another under the watchful eye of the wealthy crowd.

Maggie lowered her voice. "I'm going to say good night. When you can get away, I'll be waiting in my cabin."

She bowed a thank you and headed to her room.

She had Bella call for a hot bath and pour a spicy sandalwood scent soap into the warm tub. She stripped off her clothes and slid into the water. When he arrived, Bella show Maggie's visitor in the door. Connor stepped into the private cabin, he found her with one leg dangling out of the tub and a frothy sponge in her hand.

"Care to join me?" she asked.

He hurried out of his formal clothes and Maggie stood as he stepped into the big copper tub. He kissed her deeply.

The water amplified the heat of the contact, as she ran her wet hands up his long, lean body. Maggie stopped him before he lowered himself into the water, she crouched to kiss his growing erection. She opened her mouth and took in the hardening tip, rubbing her tongue over the head, his knees buckled and as he reached out and grabbed the shelf on the wall of the cabin for support. She slowly worked his manhood into her mouth and deeper into her throat. She took her time as he groaned, and ran his free hand through her loose hair. His hips bucked as he pushed even deeper.

"Oh, bloody hell, woman. You're driving me wild."

Maggie took the base of his now fully hard member and continued to work his penis in and out of her wet mouth, over and over. She massaged his balls in her hands and he arched his back, letting out a moan of deep desire. She could feel his gonads tighten. She slipped him out of her mouth and pulled him to her.

He started to part her legs but Maggie stopped him and pushed him into the tub. She straddled his body and lowered herself onto his swollen shaft. She began to rock back and forth, tightening her inner muscles to pump his rock hard flesh. She arched her back and Connor caught her nipple between his lips, then gently nipped them with his teeth.

Maggie gasped and picked up her pace, riding him hard until she climaxed. She bore down harder and Connor hammered into his own orgasm.

Later, in her warm bed, Maggie lay in the circle of his arms, swirling her fingers through the golden hair on his forearm. He had made love to her slowly, thoroughly and with so much deliberate care Maggie hardly knew what to say to him. She had been with many men, some kind, even loving, some harsh and selfish, but they all had one thing in common: they were clients. Even Race, to some extent was a part of her business. He had been her partner and at one time her client. This man was not a client, not a paying customer. She wasn't in love with him, and she didn't know him well enough to know if she liked him. He was charming, handsome, and very, very good in bed. Anything more was still a mystery.

Connor sighed in his sleep and pulled her naked body closer to his. She liked the feel of him, liked the way his chest rose and fell under her. She loved the spicy smell of his skin and the strength in his hands. She turned his hand over and looked at it. There were no cuts or calluses, it was smooth and the nails were clean and well-shaped. She found herself comparing them to Race's hands. They were so different, but still the hands of a man.

He moaned and yawned and slowly came awake. "Is it morning?"

"No. The sun won't be up for hours."

He started to move but Maggie held on to him. "Can you stay awhile?"

He started to kiss her shoulder but Maggie stopped him. "I meant, can we talk?"

"Of course." He held her tight and snuggled in. "What do you want to talk about?"

"I'd like to get to know you, Connor."

His golden brows furrowed. "I'm not sure what to say. I like you Maggie. You're very different from any lady I've ever known. But I'm not a very interesting man."

"Are you trying to convince me or you?"

He chuckled but pulled her closer. "I doubt I could convince you to do anything you didn't want to do. I am truly happy that I've gotten to know you and enjoy your company."

"Why don't you think you're interesting?" she asked pulling herself as close to his warm body as she could.

He shrugged a broad shoulder. "I'm a lie, an actor pretending to be someone I'm not. You are a real, flesh and blood woman, living a fascinating life. I have nothing to compare with that."

"I think you're fascinating. You're a knight looking for a princess to rescue you. I hope you find her."

They made love again, Connor leaving her weary and sated. He was an expect lover, able to draw out her pleasure and his own from brief moments to endless minutes of intense bliss. He slipped from her room before dawn and Maggie curled up to sleep like the dead.

Maggie determined to spend her last two days on ship away of the overwhelming charms of the charming British Lord. She accepted every invitation she received from Emily and Mrs. Aberson and even lunch with Captain Graham. She wasn't avoiding him, exactly. But she didn't want him to think she might be his princess. She missed him at night. Her body ached for his touch and throbbed for his body pounding into hers.

She joined the ladies for lunch, enjoying the sun and the chance to wear her light jacket and stylish hat. It was lovely and even the conversations, bland as they were, were pleasant. Maggie had not enjoyed the company of women of this class since her childhood and it was enjoyable, even as the subject of Connor Grant came up.

"He has an impeccable pedigree, and an ancient family lineage." Mrs. Aberson said again trying to win Maggie over to Connor's plight. "And while I do not improve of colonials marrying into the peerage, I can make the exception for a young lady such as yourself."

"For me?" Maggie felt as if she suddenly didn't speak the same language.

"May I ask you a very personal question," Emily Markel asked. "Are you a buccaneer?"

"A buccaneer?" Maggie had no idea what she was talking about.

"It's not uncommon." Mrs. Aberson sounded like a primary school teacher. "Wealthy, American families send their daughters to the continent looking for penniless, titled men desperate to save their estates and family names. Everyone gets what they want and go on to live happy lives. That is why Carrick was in New York, looking for a suitable young woman."

"And what about love?" Maggie asked. "What about companionship?"

"Love can come with time, my dear. Now, are you interested in the Earl of Carrick?" Mrs. Merkel asked with a laugh.

Maggie didn't know how to answer.

"If you have a mind to catch him," Mrs. Aberson continued as if she were instructing her. "You should do it now, before we land. It will doubtless save you a lot of work."

Maggie wondered if she could ask the Earl of Carrick if he was wooing her for her money. The idea made her laugh. She had sold herself for money all her life to the scorn of decent society. Now, she had met a man doing exactly the same thing with a wink and a nod from the very same society.

She would make it a point to ask Connor Grant if it was the reason behind his seduction. Was it her body or her purse he wanted to enjoy?

Emily rolled her eyes. "We sound so cold-blooded, but it really is a fine way for everyone to get what they need. You should consider all this. He is a fine catch."

Maggie locked her door that night and turned out the light, ignoring her lover's light tapping when it came. She needed to think, to understand her own head on this. She had only meant to have fun, to take a handsome man to her bed while she traveled to a new place. She had no idea she might pick the one man who could want more than a few nights of sex.

And the worst part was: she liked him. Connor Grant was fun, and she needed some fun.

She tossed and turned all night, dreaming of hot kisses, a hard body, and blue eyes which seemed to see past her shields to her very soul. He was different, but she was still Maggie MacGregor, a madam from a small Colorado boomtown. She was no New York City heiress. She was not marrying material. She was no one's savior. And no matter how understanding his society was about a man marrying for money, who he married was still a matter of social decree. A madam was no choice, no matter how rich she was.

She ate her breakfast in her room, other than lunch with Emily and dinner at Captain Graham's table. She did her best to avoid Connor Grant, other than the few times they bumped into each other. And once the ship docked, she determined she would do well to stay away from the handsome Earl all together.

Mrs. Merkel, who seemed more determined than ever to make friends with Maggie, insisted Maggie visit her home in London. They could enjoy the rest of the season with the Markels, her new friend suggested, before Maggie and Bella moved on to Paris or Madrid.

Maggie agreed, and in an instance she was the center of the Markel's social world. And it didn't keep her away from Lord Grant, who was a fixture on the London scene. It wasn't exactly what she has expected, but it was a far cry from the society of her brothel.

June 1st 1884

I find myself more intrigued by my Lord Lover, than I have been with any man since Race. I find it enjoyable and terrifying at the same time. I have been a long time holding my heart at arm's length and I am not ready to risk it being broken again. And I'm afraid that despite having welcomed him into my bed with so much enthusiasm, when he finds out who and what I am, he will break my heart....

The Belgravia area of London was a posh neighborhood filled with beautiful homes. Hyde Park was nearby where Emily and Maggie went for a ride in her Victoria, the carriage which Emily took great pride in driving herself.

Maggie took lunch and met the stylish people who flocked to the city to see and be seen. She learned the social rules from the women who lived them as if they were the Ten Commandments. Even though the need for such formalities would not follow her home to Sinners Creek, it was fun to practice them. "When in Rome," she told herself.

She ordered beautiful handcrafted calling cards,

which she left behind when visiting with Emily, lace fans and white gloves, which she was never without. Most of the time, she thought it was funny, a little silly and certainly fussy, but it was also fun pretending she was part of the stylish crowd.

She had been enjoying Emily's hospitality for two weeks when she returned from a morning of paying compliments, the social visits the upper crust paid one another every morning, and found a surprise waiting for her. Among the calling cards waiting for the popular Miss McGregor, was one of an elegant cream color with raised lettering. She ran her finger over the name.

Lord Connor Grant. The Earl of Carrick.

She felt heat suffuse her face and moisture pool between her legs at the very thought of him. He'd been here. He had found her, and he was calling on her like a proper suitor.

Emily looked over her shoulder and gave her arm a playful nudge. "See. What did I tell you?"

July 2nd 1884

Receiving Connor's calling card gave me a thrill like I have never had before. It was wicked and fun and sexy, in the most secretive way possible. I will not seek him out but I am sure we will meet and when we do, I will be face to face with temptation itself....

Maggie sat in the window seat watching the rain fall. It was always nice when the weather cooperated with her bad moods. The traffic was usually brisk this early in the morning, especially considering the rain. She was looking out the side of the house over the garden and it was impossible to look at the dripping wisteria and not think about Connor.

She had missed him. But the thought of sitting in the Markel's stylish parlor sipping tea and making polite conversation, while imaging his sleek body pounding a hard rhythm into the hungry folds of her womanhood was more than she thought she could stand.

Mr. Phillips, the Markel's dour butler stepped in with the silver tray. A single card lay in the center. Maggie recognized the cream colored card with the raised lettering. She knew what it said before she picked it up.

Connor.

"The gentleman is waiting in the entry. Do you wish for me to send him in?

Maggie chewed her lip. She wasn't ready. She needed more time, and she needed Emily to keep her mind off the delicious way he made her body feel.

"Tell Lord Grant the family is out."

The butler walked away and Maggie turned to watch the rain.

Later that day, Emily returned and asked why Maggie didn't receive Connor Grant.

"I wasn't in a mood for company."

Emily smiled. "I hope that changes. My husband has suggested a dinner party and Grant will be included."

The party was a huge success, Emily was eager to introduce Maggie to her London friends and to open her to polite society. Maggie wasn't certain she wanted to be so exposed but her new friend seemed eager to conduct the whirlwind of the season. Maggie wondered if Emily was bored. She had a large house but many servants to run it for her, a cook and personal maid. She had no business to run and Maggie wasn't sure shopping and visiting was as fulfilling as she pretended.

But the people were very gracious to Maggie and many of the women were downright friendly. The men were more guarded but she often saw them looking at her as if they were all imagining her naked. That was never uncommon but in this setting it was a little unnerving.

When Carrick arrived with a handful of friends, Maggie was formally introduced to them all and accepted their fine compliments. And, if Connor lingered a moment too long while kissing her hand, no one suspected his kiss send a thrill through her.

Emily purposely sat them together at dinner and after brandy and cigars, the men joined the women in the large evening parlor. Connor sat next to her as some of the younger ladies played the pianoforte and sang.

At the end of the night, Connor escorted Maggie to the door where the butler and several footmen waited with their coats. Before he left, Connor slipped a note in her hand, and kissed her knuckles in parting.

In her room, Maggie opened the note.

My dear friend,

I dream about you. Your perfect body and fiery kisses haunt me. The touch of your heated skin fills my sleep and I wake hard and hungry for you. Please, do not torture me. Find a way to come to me, and I will make you sing.

C.

It was risqué, a lover's letter, filled with intimacies Maggie couldn't let anyone else see. She hid it in her journal and dreamed of her lover's body pressed to hers.

July 9th 1884

I have been invited to join the Markels at a ball. I have ordered a dress and I swear Bella is more excited about the party, than I am. I am excited about the prospect of seeing Connor. I ache for him and I must find a way to have him again....

At Lady Crestwell's ball, Maggie had danced with the second son of the Duke of Edgecomb and Lord Gresson. She had accepted a cup of punch from some stuffy little Earl and had managed to avoid the attentions of half the peerage of the United Kingdom. She was taking a break on a settee with Emily when Colin walked into Lady Rossi's ballroom.

She felt like the air had been sucked out of the room, and the suffocating heat that had only a minute ago been barely noticeable, now seemed to overwhelm her. Her thighs began to twitch and her body to ache at the sight of him.

He crossed the room and stopped before her, sketching a small bow before taking her hand and helping her to her feet. "Miss McGregor, may I have the next dance?"

"I would like that, Lord Grant."

He led her to the dance floor and into a mazurka and then without letting her go, into a waltz. He held her shockingly close. The hand he held and the small of her back where his other hand rested, seemed to sizzle. Her body all but throbbed every time his leg brushed hers. She felt his gaze skim over her, taking in the curve of her flushed cheeks and the dip of her neckline.

"Another dance and you'll ruin my reputation completely," she said.

The music came to a trembling finish and Maggie felt as though she might orgasm with the slightest provocation.

"Then perhaps we should find a cooler place to talk."

He got them both a glass of cordial and led her to the moonlit garden. They strolled along a path lined with roses and night blooming jasmine. The heady scent made her dizzy. She felt as if she were already drunk.

"So how do you like London?" he asked, leading her across the lawn to an arbor which overlooked a small woods. The arbor was dripping with blooming wisteria and made them invisible to the house.

"I am enjoying myself very much," she said, taking a seat in beneath the flowered bower.

"Admit it." Connor said joining her. "You're happy to see me."

She smiled as he moved closer, his finger brushing her cheek. It sent shivers down her back.

"I am happy to see you," she said, moving closer. "More than happy."

She tipped her head as his mouth found hers. Maggie captured his face in her hands and kissed him deeply, tasting the cordial on his tongue and the whiskey he had swallowed before. His kiss was intoxicating and she slipped closer. He trailed hot kisses down her throat and over her chest.

"We might be discovered here," she whispered.

"No," he breathed against her skin. "This was built by the former lady of the house. She met her lover, the under gardener here. No one comes near it now."

He slid the sheer cap sleeves off her shoulder. Maggie wiggled her shoulder, freeing her breasts to his greedy mouth. He suckled one pink nipple and rolled the other between his fingers. Maggie gasped and threw back her head, letting him have his way with her flesh. Maggie was on fire and knew there was only one thing would quench that fire... and that was to take him here and now. She stood up and carelessly lifted her skirts to her thighs; she straddled his legs. Connor fumbled with the buttons of his pants and opened the fly of his trousers.

He was already growing hard and it took no time at all for Maggie to stoke him to his full length. He slid his hand into the slit in the crotch of her silk pantaloons. Maggie groaned as his finger delved into her wet folds.

"You did miss me," he said and Maggie laughed as moved forward and took his hard cock into herself.

He groaned as Maggie began to rock back and forth, pumping him as hard as she could. She rode him hard, glorying in the pressure building quickly. His mouth on her breasts, his hard member throbbing inside her and she tightened her muscles around him. His hands pulled her buttocks apart and he applied a gentle pressure to the rim of her anus. It added to the pressure and she reached between her legs to slip her fingers around the base of his dick. She did as he had showed her before, applying pressure to the thick vein which supplied blood to his member. The pressure ebbed and flowed, each time taking them higher and higher until he reared up and slammed against her engorged flesh. His orgasm was so hard, Maggie felt like she was riding a wild horse, until she climaxed and collapsed onto him.

"I missed you." She kissed him softly and began to right her dress.

Connor tucked himself away and then helped her rearrange her clothes.

"You know," he said putting her embroidered shawl modestly around her shoulders. "If we were husband and wife, we could have this for the rest of our lives."

Maggie stopped. "Are you asking me to marry you?"

"Yes."

She started to walk away and Connor hurried to catch her. "It's a ridiculous idea."

"Why is it ridiculous? We like each other. We certain enjoy each other."

"I am not the one to rescue you, Connor."

"This is not about money. Well, not just about money."

"It's not?" She said, sounding far angrier than she was.

"No," he said with surprising conviction. He caught her arms and stopped her. "Look at us. We can't stop touching each other. We know each other and we have fun together. There is nothing wrong with that."

"I never thought there was. But there is something about me you don't know."

"I don't care," he insisted.

Maggie stopped on the limestone walkway and squared her shoulders. "I do not own a ladies school, and I am not the daughter of a wealthy horse breeder. I owned two of the finest saloon and brothels in Colorado."

Connor looked stunned and then confused. "You mean you are a--"

"I'm a madam."

His eyes grew wide but he said nothing.

"Good night, my lord." Maggie gave him her sweetest smile, then turned and walked away. A part of her was sad that he did nothing to stop her. But it was for the best.

It was over and she could go on with her plans to see the world.

July 10th 1884

I am certain I have seen the last of the Earl of Carrick. It makes me a little sad and a little relieved at the same time. I am who I am. I can't be a gentlewoman, no matter how fun it is to pretend. I will see the world, have my fun, and go back to Sinners Creek....

Maggie did her best to pretend she was fine. But Bella could see through her. The morning after the dance, the cagey older woman did her best to cheer her up.

"So the little assistant cook asks me; are all ladies maid, in America, Negros? I say, sweet as you please; no, but all assistant cooks are." She heehawed with laughter. "Her eyes get big as saucers until Mrs. Doolittle, the head cook starts to laugh. Pretty soon, the whole room is busting a gut. But I don't think that old butler, fella thought it was funny."

Maggie chuckled and Bella went back to fluffing her dress.

"Box all these dress up and send them back to Opal. They will fit her and I don't want them anymore." She waved a hand at the collections of dresses she had pulled from her armoire and hung on the garment rack.

"She's gonna think it's Christmas," Bella said.

"If fact, box up all those ones too." Maggie gestured to all the dresses in one of the closets. "And leave a note to have Hattie alter them to fit all the girls. I doubt Harry has thought to update any of their clothes lately."

"It's going to leave you a little scarce on dresses, ain't it?"

"Then we'll need to go to the dressmaker's. I need a change and I might as well start with my clothing."

Maggie got dressed and the two set out to the couturière. She picked out several new, more modest patterns and some fabric for new walking and day dresses. Then, moved to the evening and ball dresses. Again she chose the more modest dresses and matching accessories.

Bella held up a rather matronly dress of russet brown silk. "Is this part of the new you?"

"It's just a dress."

When they returned to the house, Mr. Phillips met her with the small silver tray.

In the privacy of her room, Maggie broke the seal and opened the note.

My Dearest Friend.

*I know my reaction to your confession at the ball
was less than gentlemanly. I hope you have not sworn off me.
I still wish to make you my wife. I have grown fonder of you
than any woman I have ever known.*

*Please allow me to visit you this afternoon, and plead the
case for our continued connection.*

I am, as ever, your dearest friend.

C.

Maggie folded the note and put it into her pocket.
She liked the idea that what she did—who she was—
didn't matter to the likes of the Earl. But the reality was
that it would matter. He might want to have sex with
her again, but was it what she wanted? She had not
come to England just to find a lover. She had a chance
at something new, something better and she wanted it
enough to work for it. The modest clothes were a start
but did she have to cut ties with The Earl of Carrick.
She had been a gentleman's daughter once upon a time,
before the Deacon, before Jackson and the men who
had followed. She had nearly been a wife. Bless Race
for seeing her as someone who could change. And she
could be a gentlewoman again. But she had to do it on
her own.

She sat at the writing table and opened the ink
well.

My Dearest Friend,

While I hope what you said is true. I cannot see how, knowing what you know about my past, we can consider marriage. I do appreciate your company and I am fond of you. If you wish to visit this afternoon, I am certain it will be acceptable.

Your Dear Friend.

M.

Emily Markel was back from her morning visits and waiting with Maggie when the Earl arrived. They had tea and enjoyed an unusual day of warmth and sunshine in the garden and chatted, like normal people. The afternoon passed pleasantly and ended, as these days often did, with a plan for another day. Carrick invited Maggie and the Markels to a night at the theater in his private box.

Maggie had been to the theater in New York, but this trip was about more than just watching a play. Maggie was very aware that everyone was as busy watching each other as they were the actors on stage. Everyone wanted to see who the pretty girl was sharing space with the handsome Earl.

At intermission, the Markels discreetly excused themselves to get refreshments, leaving the two of them alone.

"Is this proper?" Maggie asked, looking around at the dozen or so sets of eyes watching them.

"It's perfectly fine. It's like dancing at a ball."

"As I recall, those innocent dances led to a less than innocent tête-à-tête, and the entire night ended in an unmitigated disaster."

His blond brow furrowed. "I'm sorry about my reaction. You just surprised me."

"Society would have deemed my behavior that of a whore; is it such a surprise I might actually be a prostitute, a soiled dove, a working girl?" she whispered.

"I don't care about any of that."

"Everyone cares about all of that." She tried to smile but she knew it had to look as empty as it felt.

"Am I like all the men you've known before? Have I treated you as anything but a friend? I like you Maggie, as I said, more than I have ever liked another woman. I am not single at thirty because I have never met a woman who society wouldn't approve of or had deep enough pockets to save my estate? I'm single because I've never met a woman I liked enough to marry, even if she had the means to save me."

She chewed her lip but she couldn't find anything to say to him.

"I'm telling the truth, just like you did. Now, whether or not you walk away is up to you. But I hope you'll stay and let me get to know you."

He seemed so sincere. Maggie actually found herself hoping he meant it.

They enjoyed the rest of the play and Maggie only smiled when Emily invited the Earl to dinner the next night.

July 17th 1884

I admit my feelings for Connor Grant have begun to change. He has dined with us nearly every night for more than a week. It is apparent to everyone he is courting me and while I am still doubtful anything can come of this flirtation, it is fun to pretend I can have a different life. Bella encour-

ages me and swears she will be happy in England, but I am still not convinced....

Connor was always the last to leave any event they attended together. He lingered while holding her hand. He whispered how much he missed her. How he dreamed about her. He kissed her hand; occasionally he turned her hand over and kissed her uncovered wrist. His warm touch sent a thrill through her body to pool between her legs. He made her body hot with need. She did her best to play demure, to pretend she was unaffected by his nearness but it was a lie.

She still wanted him.

Other men came to court her. But they left her cold. And all the while the shadow of Race King seemed to haunt her. She compared Connor to Race, and always she wondered if she had had her only love, if there was even a chance of feeling that way again.

She sat on the window seat overlooking the rainy street below. She reread her journals wrapping herself in the memory of the man who had truly loved her for her.

"You visiting with Mr. Race again?" Bella asked.

She closed the book, unwilling to share him, even with Bella.

"You going out today?" Bella asked, hanging her freshly cleaned and pressed dress into the wardrobe.

"No, I believe Emily is going out to see Lady Bartell. I'm just going to stay put and rest. It's been a whirlwind and I'm getting tired."

Bella straightened the items on her dressing table, and for a moment Maggie's mind was back in Sinners Creek. She had come so far, and thought it would be a lark, easy to go back to what she had known before. But would it? She was proud of her life back home but at the same time, the people here treated her with so much respect. She was a lady, not a common whore, and she liked that feeling.

"How do you know you'd be happy staying here in England with me? It's different from back home."

Bella took a deep breath. "It rains a lot here. But the people below stairs are good and honest folks. I made a huge change going from Louisiana to Colorado, and I can make this change too. If you wanna stay, I'm all for it. But you gotta be happy. I ain't staying to see you open some fancy English house. If it's just for money then we might as well go on back home."

Maggie smiled at her and hugged her tight.

"This is the sort of thing you can't do here." Bella complained but smiled and patted Maggie back.

In the afternoon, Phillips escorted Connor into the dayroom and Maggie felt her heart begin to pound at the sight of him. His blond hair was damp from the rain but his smile was sunny, setting off the little crinkles at the corner of his eyes. It made her smile. She could see him so clearly. Handsome rogue, sincere suitor, loyal husband, dedicated father, he really wasn't a mystery, not to her.

"Should I ring for tea or would you prefer a cordial?"

"It's just you and I, Maggie," he said, taking the seat too close to her. "Can we just talk, like two people, two friends?"

She smiled at him and turned, taking his hands in hers. It was the sort of thing she couldn't do with the eyes of society watching them. "Can I get you a whiskey? I think Simon has some in the liquor cupboard."

"No," he said, bringing her hands to his mouth. "Being alone with you is all the intoxication I need. Oh, it is good to really talk to you. I get so sick of hearing people chatter about clothes and carriages. Let's talk about something real."

"What's real? I feel like I woke up in a dream and nothing is real," she said. "Tell me about your world. Your real world."

"My real world is Colton Manor. My home in Surrey."

"Is it beautiful?" She did pour him a cup of tea.

He smiled. "It was."

She sat close enough to smell the woodsy scent of his cologne. "It's not now?"

"Oh the land is lovely and the house sound, but it's not what it was when my grandfather ran it. My father was…"

"I've heard the story of your father."

He smiled knowingly. "I'm sure you have. But my grandfather was a wonderful manager. He loved the land and the people who worked it. He would have loved you."

She laughed.

"He told me years ago to find a girl who had spirit. I would never regret marrying a girl with courage and pluck."

"And you think I have pluck?"

"I think you might be the pluckiest girl I've ever met." He reached out and touched her cheek.

Maggie leaned into the touch and reveled in the heat of his hand. "Conner. I want you to know I do want you. I think about you all the time and I—"

He drew her to him sharply, kissing her hard. There was such a needy edge to the contact, an almost desperate quality took over as he moved his mouth roughly along her neck and lower, to the edge of her neckline. Maggie was so overwhelmed by the passion rising in her, she had to clear her head and push him away.

She crossed the room on wobbly legs, but nearly sighed with relief when she found a lock for the door. She slipped it into place and opened the small buttons of her blouse as she turned. Connor met her in the middle of the room and roughly took her to the side of the small fireplace.

Maggie hurried to open the buttons of his pale gray trousers. She had no idea how badly she had wanted him until his mouth descended to the peak of her left nipple and he sucked it into his mouth. He lolled the fresh with his tongue, making her gasp with pleasure.

She freed him from his trousers and despite the delicious sparks which seems to radiate from her nipple in all directions she moved down and took his hard penis into her hungry mouth. She couldn't see much above her but he gripped the mantel of the fireplace as she began to pleasure him with her tongue. She reached up, and found the edges of his perfectly tailored shirt. She slipped her fingers into the fabric and found the taut skin over his flat belly. She slid her hand up, rubbing her hands over the beautiful body she couldn't see. He groaned his longing and rocked his hips to move him in and out of her mouth. He cupped her cheek and ran his hand along her jaw as it opened wider to accommodate his length.

His knees nearly buckled and Maggie worked her way along the stiff shaft, licking and kissing, blowing out a puff of hot breath and sending him nearly out of his mind. Finally, he pulled her roughly to her feet and yanked her dress up her thighs. Maggie nearly screamed as her parted her legs and buried himself deep into her wet folds. She was surprised how close she was to orgasm herself. He hammered into her, and though she knew he was trying to be as quiet as possible, he said her name over and over.

Each thrust took Maggie higher until she wrapped her legs around him and let him push her into the wall. She arched her back and the position of his hard dick shifted inside her. In no time at all he was thrusting even deeper and Maggie came in a shattering orgasm. Connor followed with two more deep thrusts and then nearly sagged to the floor.

All that held her up was his strong arms and the will not to ruin her already wrinkled dress.

He hurried to tuck himself away and helped her redo the buttons on her collar before he handed her the last of his whiskey and unlocked the door, before taking a seat at a respectful distance. In a few moments, the sounds of voices drifted in ahead of Simon and Emily Markel.

"Carrick," Simon said as Connor came to his feet to meet them.

"I'm sorry to drop in unannounced. I was hoping to extend an invitation. I had hoped you would all join me at Colton for a weekend holiday."

Emily nearly squealed and Simon offered a smile and a handshake. "Of course, old man. We would be delighted."

"Miss McGregor, can I count on your lovely presence as well?" Connor asked with a gleeful twinkle in his eyes.

Maggie had a hard time not laughing. She was still reeling from the fury of their sex and he was politely offering a proper invitation to a party. "Of course, Lord Grant, I'd love a visit to your home."

After Connor left, Emily was nearly giddy with excitement. Simon Markel's wealth had been made in trade and an invitation to a private party with a member of the peerage, even one in financial crisis was a boon to his status.

Emily turned to Maggie and squeezed her arm. "This is no doubt all because of you."

For a moment, Maggie panicked. Had Phillips noticed the locked door? Had he said something to Emily about Maggie's conduct? She knew it wasn't likely. She took a deep breath.

"He is quite in love with you, my dear."

Maggie only smiled. The idea of it made her happier than she could say.

June 20th 1884

We arrived at Colton Manor and I am nearly breathless by the beauty of this area. The rolling hills and lush green fields remind me of Ohio. The house is much as he described it. But he failed to mention it is a seventeenth century castle with three floors and towers which soar into the clear blue sky. Rows of windows glitter in the sunlight, each topped with a graceful stone arch. Any woman would feel like a princess in such an amazing castle....

The Markels and their American visitor were not the only guests at the house for the weekend. They arrived late on Thursday and found Connor had rounded up a collection of impressive titles and family to make it an event which would, no doubt be talked about in the papers for weeks. One of his aunts, Flora Grant, a round little thing with pink cheeks and steely gray hair, grinned from ear to ear as she was introduced to Maggie. It made her wonder what they had all been told about her.

Maggie didn't see a lack of money in the beautiful furnishings and fine appointments to Colton Manor. There were at least a half-dozen young footmen, and a butler riding rough-shod over them all. She was certain there had to be at least a dozen people they didn't see, plus a cook staff. Everyone cast a sidelong look at Bella as she was led to Maggie's room along with her cases.

Maggie got Connor to the side. "Is Bella going to be welcomed by your staff?"

"Of course, have no fear there. They have never seen a Negro but they are all good and decent people. And Mrs. Guthrie will make her welcome."

She was introduced to a lot of people before dinner, including Connor's oldest friend, Billy Brathwaite and his younger brother Carlson. Billy was full of stories of his and Connor's school days at Eaton, and Connor's aunts, Flora and Edith Bingley talked about his childhood and how dear he had been to the childless women.

After the third set of testimonials it became very clear everyone was there to convince Maggie what a wonderful man, Connor was. She didn't doubt them and she really enjoyed the stories but it began to bother

her that she couldn't share much of her life.

No one was tactless enough to ask her outright about her wealth but she was certain most of the collected group had a good idea of her worth, if not how she got the money.

The first two evenings were filled with chatter, and punctuated with impromptu musical performances and a brief reading of some particularly bad poetry. Finally, the eyes of the collective group turned to Maggie.

"Play the piano for us, Maggie." Emily said pulling her toward a lovely grand. "Something happy."

Maggie thought for a moment and began playing a tune from Pirate of Penzance. Race had gotten her the sheet music two years earlier and she had seen the play in New York. It always made her smile, and she played it often in the saloon. At first, the crowd seemed shocked by the wildly lively song and Maggie realized, Emily probably meant something more classical but soon enough Connor's aunt, a great theater buff, began to sing along and the awkward moment was gone and everyone was joining in.

The evening passed and Maggie was relieved. As Connor walked her to her room, Maggie apologized for the gaffe.

"Think nothing of it," he said, taking her arm and chucking her chin. "I think everyone was charmed by it. And your rendition of Mendelssohn's 'Spring' was quiet beautiful."

"I think you would forgive me anything."

"Maggie, I've fallen hopelessly in love with you. It's easy to see only your perfection."

His words stunned her. He loved her. Had he said it out loud? She looked up at his handsome face and smiled. "You can't mean that."

"I love you. I can and I do mean it. I have looked my whole life for a woman who could be my match, heart, soul, body. We are a match, Maggie. Smart, strong, maybe a bit mercenary. And we want the same things. To have a good life. We can give each other those things. And in bed. I haven't even begun to show you the things I've learned. I can make your beautiful body sing."

She knew he meant every word and the heat in his eyes melted her tough core. He was her match, more than any man, even Race had ever been. But would she really fit in? Could a simple saloon girl really become a great lady, the princess in a grand castle?

"Please," he said, lifting her hand to his mouth. "Think about it tonight, dream about my kisses and tomorrow I will ask you formally to be my wife." He kissed her knuckles, then turned her hand over, slowly slipped off her glove and pressed a warm kiss to the palm of her hand.

"I will think about it. But there is one thing that we haven't talked about."

"Any subject is open"

"Money."

He frowned. "Money?"

"There has been a lot of talk, about your debts, the state of your finances and your estate." She pulled her hand from his grasp. "I know you need money to make your estate right."

"Yes, I do."

"If I were poor, a poor working girl without a dollar to my name. Would you feel this way?"

He took a deep breath and seemed to sigh it out

with effort. "Everything you've said is true. And yes, a rich wife will save my ass. But the truth is, the brutal truth is, if you were a poor woman, I would have never met you. You are rich. We have met and I am more than grateful that the Almighty would send me such a savior."

He waited for her reply but Maggie felt suddenly speechless. Maggie smiled and wished him good night, then slipped into her room.

Bella was busy readying her nightgown and bed.

"You have a good evening, Miss Maggie?"

"I think I had the best evening of my life." Maggie nearly sighed. "Connor wants to marry me. He is going to formally ask me tomorrow."

"Hallelujah! I was praying he might get around to that. Wait, he's going to ask you formal-like. But he already told you he was going to ask?" She laughed. "These Brits are a funny bunch. You gonna say yes, right?"

Maggie said nothing.

"Oh, Miss, please think about this."

"I am thinking about it. I am a saloon whore, he is an English Lord," she said emphatically.

Bella waved a hand to stop her. "Hang on there. He's got a few skeletons in his closet too. His grandmother was his grandfather's mistress until she got pregnant with his daddy. His daddy lost the whole family fortune on gambling and a greedy mistress named Minnie. And Connor is in debt to everyone and every store in most of England. You're practically a saint compared to them."

"How do you know all that?"

"All the folks downstairs have to do is talk, and they are good at it."

Maggie crossed the room and hugged her. "You think I should marry him and save him."

"I think you two ought to marry and save each other."

Bella helped her undress and ready for bed. Then Maggie kissed her friend's cheek and settled in for the night.

Bella was right, they could save each other. And Connor was right, if she was anyone but who she was, if she hadn't been sailing first class, she would never have met him. So did that mean she was exactly where she was meant to be? Or was she trying so hard to find a way to make it all okay?

She dreamt of Race that night. He was sitting by the fire in their little cabin. He was sipping a glass of whiskey and watching the fire crackle. He looked up at her once and smiled.

She asked him what she should do and he reached out and took her hand. "If you love someone, helping them is easy."

He went back to watching the fire and after a while she noticed his chair was empty. But amazingly, she didn't feel sad.

The sound seemed to merge with her dream, a thump followed by a second and a muffled curse. It was the latter that brought her fully awake. Maggie sat up in the bed and tried to focus in the thin strip of light coming from the lights in the hallway. Her door was open.

"Connor?"

The words were barely out of her mouth when she knew it wasn't Connor or Bella stumbling around in the darkness of her room.

"I know who you are." The voice that answered her was wavering and the words slurred; whoever it was, he was very drunk.

Maggie lit the candles on her nightstand and the face at the foot of her bed confused her.

Carlson Braithwaite swayed on unsteady legs. "Hello there, Maggie."

"You should go back to your bed, Mr. Braithwaite," she said softly and hurried to find a robe. She rose from her bed and crossed to the door pushing it wider. "Leave please."

"But I know who you are and I have ten pounds for a night with the Silver Filly herself."

When it dawned on her what he had said, a frisson of fear snaked down her back.

He knew!!

Maggie closed the door with a soft click. "I don't know what you think you know, but we have never met."

"But I still know who you are. I thought you looked familiar and then you started to play that song. I was in a saloon one night, while on tour in America and the very pretty whore who owns it, played the same tune." He began to hum and dance around the room. He tripped over the bench of the dressing table and tipped a bottle of perfume. It teetered for a moment and fell to the floor with a crash.

"I want you to leave," Maggie snapped.

He continued to dance toward her. "Come on, give us a little kiss, a little taste of what you've been feeding my brother's friend. Isn't my money good enough for you?"

"You've made a mistake."

"No!" he shouted. "Now be a good girl. Come here and get your clothes off."

He lunged at her, catching the lace of her silk robe and tearing the thin fabric. The strap of her gown broke too, and her shoulder and her left breast were exposed to his leering gaze. Maggie grabbed her robe and pulled it closed, just as Braithwaite launched himself at her again. He wrapped her in a bear hug, pressing a wet kiss to her face. Maggie tried to push away.

The smell of the liquor on his breath made her sick and angry. She slammed her elbow into his ribs. Braithwaite made a "woofing" sound and released her. He made another grab for her. Maggie tried to duck out of his way but he caught her hair. "Stop fighting me. I'm not going to hurt you. I'm not taking anything you haven't given away before."

He pulled her to him, reaching around her to grope her breasts. He made a smacking sound with his mouth and tried to kiss her neck. Maggie fought, but his arms closed around her and he squeezed her breast in a punishing crush.

"Stop!" she said trying to turn out of his grasp.

A knocked rattled her door. "Maggie? Are you all right?"

"Connor!" she shouted.

There was a crash and the doorjamb splintered as Connor stormed in and grabbed Braithwaite.

He threw the man toward the door and wrapped his arms protectively around Maggie. "Carlson? What the hell is going on here?"

The noise must have awakened other visitors. The sound of their voices began to drift in. But Maggie hurried to close the door. "He knows who I am."

"I just wanna a little..." The rest of the words were lost in a drunken mumble.

"What the hell were you doing in here?" Connor asked.

Maggie pulled away from Connor and tightened her robe around her waist. "He's so drunk. He can barely stand. He said he was in my saloon. He knows who I am and he wanted to pay me."

Bella came and Maggie sent her to retrieve Billy Braithwaite.

"I could throttle you. You bastard." Connor shook the younger man hard enough to whip his head back and forth. "You come into my house and disrespect my fiancé this way."

Billy came through the door, a look of disgust on his face and Maggie braced herself for his opinion of her as well. He took hold of his brother even more roughly than Connor had.

"What have you done now, you fool?"

"He accosted Miss McGregor."

Now, it was Billy's chance to shake him. Carlson started to say something, but his brother prudently shut him up. "Enough from you! I'm sorry, Miss McGregor. If you call the carriage I'll take him to the inn at Middleson for the night."

"No, Mr. Braithwaite. There is no reason to leave."

"Take him to your room and make sure he stays there."

Billy dipped his head and all but carried his brother out the door. Connor turned as Maggie wilted to the bed. He sat next to her and Maggie felt the urge to push him away.

"Are you all right?" he asked softly.

"No." Her answer was honest. "This is how it will be, you know."

He took her hand and Maggie surprised herself by letting him. "This is not how it will be. This is one boy with a snoot-full of the last of my good cognac. I have no idea how he knows your past, or why he thought his behavior would be tolerated under any circumstances. But the very odds of anyone I know recognizing you were astronomical. And now, I think the odds of two people we know putting two and two together — actually, there are very few people in society who can even add two and two."

Maggie laughed to spite herself. "You really are an optimist, aren't you?"

"Why shouldn't I be?" he asked, gathering her close. "I believe things will always get better. Look at me. A year ago I was certain I would lose everything, my home, my dignity. Now, I have a passionate friend and lover all rolled into beautiful package."

"You called me your fiancé." She reached out and brush a loose curl from his forehead.

"I want that, Maggie, more than I ever wanted anything in my life. I want you to be my wife."

He pulled her close as he slid back putting his back to the head of her bed.

"He said some ugly things to me," Maggie said, curled into Connor's side.

"And he will pay. I can promise you."

"He's just a boy and nothing he said was a lie," she pointed out.

Connor tipped her chin up and looked into her eyes. "This isn't about the truth. A gentleman never brings up a lady's past. And accosting a woman, any woman is unacceptable. I will deal with him. And I have known William Braithwaite for twenty years, he does not want a brother this out of control."

Maggie had been through a lot. She had even had a gun put in her face once by a deranged preacher. She wasn't sure why the boy's callous words and less than damaging mauling had shaken her up so. She had been called much worse and frankly, hurt far worse, so why did this leave her rattled, and wanting to hide in her bed?

Connor shifted to his right so she could lie across his chest. She could hear the steady, solid beat of his heart and feel the heat of his body seeping through her cold limbs. He pulled a blanket from the bed and covered her.

It was him.

He was the reason this was troubling. She knew who she was, and despite her candid relationship with Connor she still didn't want him to see her as simply a saloon madam. And she never wanted to bring any shame to him. Despite being poor as a church mouse, he was a good and decent man.

But a part of her knew he was right. How many of Connor's friends could have been in her saloon. An Englishman in the Silver Filly was as unusual as a madam in high society. She wanted to believe it could never happen again.

"I will marry you, Connor."

She cuddled in closer still and let him kiss her softly and fell asleep.

June 21st 1884

I woke with Connor's arms around me and his heart beating beneath my ear. It made me feel good to find him still there but I also felt a sense of panic that the others might find him in my room. I know it's ridiculous, there is nothing chaste or proper about our relationship but I do not want to damage his name with any questionable behavior....

She hurried him out the door and called Bella to help her dress. She chose a green day dress that set off her dark hair and green eyes, and had Bella twist her hair onto her head. She came into the dining room and found a few of the guests gathered, enjoying a buffet laden with food. Maggie helped herself to bacon and fluffy eggs. The footman carried her plate and a second poured her a cup of tea and a glass of milk. She had prepared an excuse for the noise the night before but none of the guests asked her about the disturbance and she breathed a sigh of relief.

The conversation was centered on hunting and fishing. Several of the men were readying for excursion into Colton's wilds and lake. The wildlife had been long neglected and all the men were excited to cull the flocks of pheasant. The meat would go a long way to filling Colton's pantry.

Some of the ladies were putting together an outing to the south, while the others were content to wander the gardens and groves of the grounds. "You should join us, Miss McGregor," Penelope Throckmorten said. "You'll have all the time in the world to get to know Colton when you are its mistress."

Her mother chided her for her comment but Maggie only smiled at the young girl's impulsive words. And the idea struck a chord so deep in Maggie's heart, she almost gasped. Without her, this beautiful place would be sold, or turned over to the National Trust or worst yet, abandoned like some of the ruins she had seen in her travels from London. It nearly took her breath away. The injustice of it all nearly overwhelmed her.

She ate her breakfast and went to find Connor. Mr. Carter, his butler said Lord Grant was in the library with some of his guests, and then opened the heavy oak door for her.

Three men stood as she stepped inside, too late realizing the men with Connor were the Braithwaite brothers. She began to leave but it was Billy who called her back.

"I cannot express how sorry I am for my behavior last night. I was very drunk, as you know." He looked at his brother, clearly unhappy he was expected to apologize at all. "And I mistook you for... someone else."

Maggie began to say something, but Connor rose and took her hand. "Let him speak his piece, my dear."

"I am truly disgusted by my behavior."

The men all turned to Maggie for her response and she cleared her throat to stall for time.

"Thank you, Mr. Braithwaite. I fear I have a very common look, easily mistaken. Your apology is gratefully accepted."

"My brother is going to travel the continent and will be gone for some time, if he wishes to continue in my favor and enjoy the support of my estate."

Maggie felt bad for him. He was being sent away because of her. She wanted to make it better so she stepped forward and took the young man's hand. "I wish you happy trails, and hope, when you return, you will consider Connor and I your truest friends."

The look on the young man's face was one of shock. It was easy to see he had not thought Maggie would offer him her friendship. He smiled. "Thanks you, Miss. McGregor."

"You are most kind," Billy said also taking her hand in friendship. He clapped Connor on his back. "You have always been a luck son of a...." He let the epitaph hang in the air unsaid.

The brothers left them and Connor pulled her close. "You are amazing."

"I am in no position to cast stones."

He tipped her chin and kissed her mouth softly, igniting a fire inside Maggie that she loved almost as much as she loved him. And she did. She was sure of it.

"I wanted to tell you, I will accept your marriage proposal. But I will be expecting a formal offer today all the same."

He kissed her again.

April 25th 1885

The wedding was beautiful and I am so blessed to start my life with the dearest man in the world. Bella and I have settled into the manor house and the restoration of the house, which we started after our engagement, is nearly done. I surprised Connor by adding a beautiful stable to the estate. I even managed to track down an old customer of my father's, who still had horses from the bloodline my dad sold him. I was thrilled to bring the animals to Colton.

But my greatest gift to my husband arrived just in time for the wedding.

The flowers, which filled nearly every corner—some from the gardens at Colton and others brought in from as far away as London—arrived yesterday to be arranged in every room of the great house. The service was held in the courtyard on a carpet of rose petals, beneath what was the brightest, sunniest day since Maggie moved to England. Bella had dressed her in a dress of candlelight silk and ecru lace. Connor was dressed in his most becoming morning coat.

After the morning ceremony, all the collected guests gathered in the dining room for a breakfast. It was as grand as any society had ever seen.

Afterward, in her room, Maggie took a break and stared at the circle of gold on her trembling finger. She couldn't remember a time when she was happier, but, suddenly she felt tears well up in her eyes.

"You okay, girl?" Bella asked.

She swiped at her eyes. "I'm fine. These are happy tears. In fact, these are the happiest tears I've ever cried. How funny is that?"

Bella gave her a hug. "You had a hard road getting here, but here you are. You worked hard and you did it without putting another living soul down. You helped your ungrateful momma and sister, and your friends have all benefited from your hard work. So, you go on and have a happy life and no more looking back."

"I'd better get back to my guests. My new husband has a lot of things lined up for today." She smiled. "My husband. Doesn't it sound wonderful?"

Bella whipped a tear from her eye. "It does at that."

Maggie hurried down the stairs to join her guests and found her husband standing in the lobby looking for her.

"Ah, there is my bride," he called as he gathered her in his arms and kissed her.

Mr. Phillips appeared in the hallway leading a man I had not seen in nearly two years. I asked Connor to meet me in his empty den as I greeted my old friend and after a few minutes to get reacquainted, we joined my husband.

"And the sale is complete?" I asked as I led him into the room.

"Oh yes, Mr. Boater was overjoyed with the price you quoted and he is the very happy new owner of King's Inn."

"Darling, I want you to meet my former business partner, Victor Anderson. He is the purchasing officer for the new Denver Pacific Railroad and the true source of my fortune. Victor, my husband, Connor Grant, the Earl of Carrick."

"My former partner. Are we no longer partners?" he asked as he shook hands with Connor.

She kissed Victor's cheek and as usual he blushed. "I'm a married woman now, not a businesswoman, but my husband is a very clever businessman. And, of course, he is backed until he is in a more lucrative position. Now, perhaps you can explain to Connor how our arrangement works?"

"Fine," Oliver said softly. "Congratulations Lord Carrick, your wife has just made you incredibly wealthy."

"Independently wealthy," she added.

Connor seemed speechless, but gathered Maggie in his arms and kissed her soundly, making Victor blush profusely.

"I don't understand?" Connor said pulling his bride into his arms.

"I work for the Denver Pacific Railroad. I acquire land for the new rail lines."

"Our partnership was based on a bit of slight of hand," Maggie said.

"I was discussed that my company was buying the land so cheaply."

"They were terrible bullies. And the poor farmers and land owners were the ones that lost out," Maggie added.

"So I get the proposed maps for the new railways and Maggie put up the money to buy the land--"

"At a fair price." She raised a finger to punctuate her comment.

Victor gave her a smile. "She paid them at least fifty percent more to than the company was willing to play. And then she went like a lion after the railroad, getting top dollar and making a huge profit for both of us."

"It's not the most honest business but it is very profitable." Maggie said with a smile. "But I did try to help the land owners."

"But I'm still confused. How does this make me independently wealthy?" Connor asked.

"Maggie has just authorized me to make the purchases in your name, with a fifty thousand dollar wedding gift for you to take over her business."

Connor looked stunned. "But this is your business. You've worked hard to build it up."

"I am Lady Margaret Grant. I have this huge house to restore, the staff to oversee, and perhaps a child or two to rear. I will be much too busy to care about that sort of thing. And in time if you like you can pay me back my initial investment. But I'm always here if you need me."

"You are a marvel," he said softly.

"I am a wife and a very happy one. Let me ring for tea, then, we can get down to business."

ABOUT THE AUTHOR

Marcy Waldenville knew she wanted to write at an early age. A firm believer in anything-is-possible, she is happy to be following her dream.

Born and raised in a small town in Western Pennsylvania surrounded by a large and extended family. She married young and raised two wonderful children. In 2012 she added Nana to her most beloved titles. Marcy and her hubby, Kenny, live in Southern Butler County, PA with their lovable mutt, Max.

ALSO BY THIS AUTHOR

The Woodsman: Mystic Lake, Book One... Available at Amazon.

The Tears of the Damned: The Treasure Hunter Series, Book One... Available at Amazon.

The Father of the Bride... Available at Amazon in Print and Download.

Ramsey Cain... Available at Amazon.

The Confessions of a Boomtown Madam... Available at Amazon in Print and Download.

The Healing Garden, part of the **Bliss Anthology**... Available at Amazon.

The Christmas Miracle, part of the **Holiday Bliss Anthology**... Available at Amazon in Print and Download.

Made in the USA
San Bernardino, CA
08 October 2015